THE FALCON CHRONICLES: BOOK FOUR

SHARK SEAS

Also by Steve Backshall

The Falcon Chronicles

Tiger Wars
Ghosts of the Forest
Wilds of the Wolf

THE FALCON CHRONICLES: BOOK FOUR

SHARK SEAS

STEVE BACKSHALL

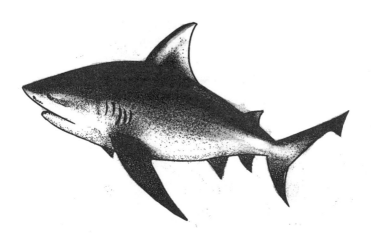

Orion
Children's Books

Orion Children's Books

First published in Great Britain in 2016 by Hodder and Stoughton

1 3 5 7 9 10 8 6 4 2

Text copyright © Steve Backshall 2016

A CIP catalogue record for this book
is available from the British Library.

ISBN: 978 1 4440 1090 9

Typeset by Input Data Services Ltd, Bridgwater, Somerset

Printed in Great Britain by Clays Ltd, St Ives plc

The paper and board used in this book are
made from wood from responsible sources.

MIX
Paper from
responsible sources
FSC® C104740

Orion Children's Books
An imprint of
Hachette Children's Group
Part of Hodder and Stoughton
Carmelite House
50 Victoria Embankment
London EC4Y 0DZ

An Hachette UK Company

www.hachette.co.uk
www.hachettechildrens.co.uk

To my mum and dad,
who made everything possible for me.

"People protect what they love."
Jacques Yves Cousteau

Meet the Characters

The Clan

Raised in ancient forests, the Clan are a secret organization, trained from birth to be thieves, fighters, renegades, spies, and even assassins. They are seemingly without morals, but bound by a common code of discipline, and loyalty to their leader, the Prophet. Though comprised of young boys, they are descended from a long line of Clan dating back generations, who have had a shadowy hand to play in some of the greatest moments of history. Each Clan boy is named for a predatory wild animal, and has a stark black tattoo of that totem animal etched on their skin. The current alpha in this lawless pack is Wolf, a rangy athlete who is fast to anger, and wields discipline just like his namesake.

Saker

Named after his totem animal the Saker falcon, Saker is comfortable with his own company, dark-eyed and browed, alert, twitchy, testy. He was a loyal servant to the Clan until his early teenage years, when he was sent on a mission to India, to capture tigers for the illegal wildlife trade, and realized the terrible nature of what he was doing. Now he is obsessed with righting wrongs against animals. His actions begin with the symbol of a carved wooden bullet, with the head of a Saker falcon embossed on the bottom. These are sent to his foes, and followed by brutal punishment. His hope is that one day merely sending someone a wooden bullet will be enough to make them change their ways.

Sinter

Sinter was born into privilege, but her mother died when she was very young, and her father tried to sell her off into an arranged marriage. She dreamed of being a doctor, and when she was kidnapped by Saker, it seemed her world was caving in. Sinter would have never chosen a life of violence, but their life on the run has given her the opportunity to live out impossible adventures. Saker imbued her with the totem animal and tattoo of a tigress, and while she may not have been brought up as Clan, she has more than a little feline fire in her veins. She is a healer at heart and a defender of the vulnerable, and longs for a time when she and Saker can fight side by side once again.

PROLOGUE

The plane taxied slowly down the runway, getting to the point where it could fire up the engines ready for takeoff. Beyond the windows, and outside the chain-link fence that surrounded the airport, was another grey, dull, depressing city. Saker was glad to be leaving. In a weird way, he was going home. In front of him, the air hostess went through the motions she had clearly done a thousand times before. She looked so glassy-eyed bored that Saker had a mind to start making silly faces at her, or to punch out the plane windows, just to see what she'd do. Anything to get her to stop her robotic performance.

There was another reason he wanted to punch the windows out. It had been a long time since he'd been on a plane. The last time, the walls of the thin metal tube had seemed to close in around him as if he was caught in a hunter's snare. Saker would have to endure many hours inside that metal tube, totally unable to affect what happened to him. If the wings fell off, or the engines caught fire, he would just have to sit there, surrounded by screaming passengers, and let some pilot he had never even met take care of things. The only thing Saker hated more than enclosed spaces was not being in control.

After all, he'd been trained from birth to be a master of manipulating events to his own advantage. Brought up as a member of the Clan, a thief and assassin for hire, his skills and talents were closely linked to his totem animal the saker falcon. The saker is a ceaselessly active bird of prey, always alert for the presence of prey, then brutal and merciless in dispatching it. Saker, for his part, could never relax; head and eyes twitching, hyper-stimulated, too aware of everything around him. He'd broken free of the Clan, and had been on the run ever since, but those years of training ran deep in his veins. He would never change what he was: a hunter, a predator. It was the search for answers that brought him here, seatbelt locking him into place in this flying prison cell. Who was he really? Where had it all begun? Who were his parents? Nothing had been easy since he'd been free; he was always running, constantly pursued, tormented by demons of events that had so nearly ended his life.

His tortured mind swirled with images of the cave in Borneo, the sinkhole where he had nearly died, locked in total darkness under a blanket of slithering and wriggling horror-show beasts. But then it got even worse, and Saker was back in the ice cave, frozen up to the waist in age-old ice. A vast polar bear was pounding on the thick ice-door of the cavern, its yellow-stained teeth dribbling saliva like melting icicles. The hairs stood up on his arms and his skin bubbled with gooseflesh.

"Saker . . ." the phantom whispered.

"NO!" He screamed and came to, inside the plane. The claustrophobia was too much. The walls were closing around him and the flight attendant was chiming her instructions like a crazed automaton, all red lip-gloss and empty eyes. The seatbelt signs *bonged* too loud, flashing like the wheels on a fruit machine. Saker screamed in terror, and started ripping at his seatbelt, his fingers suddenly useless, frostbitten to ice lollies, incapable of even the tiniest movement. Finally getting the buckle free, he leapt to his feet. There were squeals of concern from the passengers around him; the plane was mid takeoff, they were all supposed to be in their seats.

"I can't be here!" he screamed. "We need to turn the plane around!"

The Tannoy started shouting angry commands in Russian, *bing bonging* for all it was worth. If Saker had wanted to do something to attract the bored stewardess's attention, this was it! She was out of her seat like a shot, urging him to sit down, shouting at him with words he didn't understand.

"No!" he yelled yet again. "The Phantom is here! You can't lock me away, I have to get out!"

A burly passenger stood up, rocked by the pitch and roll of the plane in mid takeoff. He stood a full head taller than Saker, and looked like a man who could take care of himself. He grabbed Saker by the arm and twisted, trying to put Saker into an arm lock. Even in his feverish state, Saker's training took over; moves practised a thousand times had become as natural as taking a breath. He slipped his wrist and kept on twisting, turning the big man's arm lock against him. The man squealed in pain. Saker dropped one knee, turned and kept twisting his wrist. The big man was tossed in a neat somersault clean down the narrow aisle, and came down with a thump on his back.

The stewardess was screaming, her voice like the wind cutting through a midnight snow cave. Saker turned; he had to shut off that terrible sound. But just as he raised his hands against her, a juddering force took control of his limbs, making him leap and jump like a puppet in the hands of an overeager child. Looking down, Saker saw two needles protruding from his chest, attached to long wires. The rest of his body was not paying any attention to his commands, ferocious pain seethed through every tendon, tensing his muscles, setting his teeth into a furious chattering. His eyes could still move, and followed the wires to their source. A man in a dark suit, holding what looked like a gun; the wires ran out of it.

A Taser! He'd been Tasered! Right now fifty thousand volts were pulsing through his body. Even the biggest and toughest men can do nothing under that much force. Saker fought, but his whole body was bucking like a rodeo bull. The darkness descended, strength left his limbs and he hit the floor in between the seats. The last thing he noted before losing consciousness was that the blue carpet was thick, wiry and dirty, and he could see old trodden-in chewing gum beneath the black leather shoes of the man who had Tasered him. He heard the click of handcuffs as they closed around his wrists, and then the darkness took him.

1

The speedboat *Galeocerdo* raged across the surf towards its unseen adversary, spray spurting high from the engines dropped in a sparkling arc, painted orange and pink by the rising sun. Flying fish burst out from the surging boat, skimming across the water with their pectoral fins expanding like fans, then working like gliding wings, their tails frantically pumping side to side to drive them on. Sinter stood by the captain in *Galeocerdo*'s phone-box-sized wheelhouse, her waterproofs pulled up around her ears, keeping her knees soft to absorb the impact. A flock of gulls resting on the surface took flight at their approach, screaming out in indignant fury that their slumber should be so rudely spoiled.

The captain looked like a cliché of a salty old sea dog, with white beard and hair, a rosy red nose and a dark blue cap over eyes squinted shut from too much gazing into a reflected tropical sun. Sinter felt the fire rage in her veins as they bounced over waves towards their objective.

"We have a longline approximately three clicks ahead," he shouted, pointing at indecipherable dots on a dripping visual screen on the console. "We need to intercept before it starts getting payload."

Sinter nodded vigorously as if she understood, fighting back the urge to vomit her breakfast over the side of the boat. She'd only been out on the ocean for a few days, and hadn't yet got her sea-legs, or her sea-stomach, for that matter. Dawn raids like this one were exhilarating, but the constant bouncing was twisting her spine into knots. She was given some comfort by the fact that one of their number – an old timer who'd been doing this for years – was presently bent over the guardrail and hurling noisily into the wind, leaving behind a slick of fish food which would at least be of some benefit to the disturbed gulls.

"When we pull up on the longlines, we don't want no heroes," the captain continued, this time not only to Sinter, but to the other three oilskin-clad figures in the back of his speedboat. "The mothership is going to be cruising along at thirty knots, the line she's tailing could bounce up to twice that." Sinter strained to hear, knowing this was all vital information, but his thick Deep-South American accent and straggly white beard made it difficult to make out what he was saying. "The hooks are big enough to land a whale, let alone one of you. You get snagged by one of those and go under, I sure as hell won't be coming in to save ya."

Sinter gulped down the fear. She'd been a decent swimmer in the nice calm lake back on her father's estate in India, but that seemed a long way away now. She'd been taken from her home by force, and would never be able to return. This was about as far as you could get from the lush green of a tame old tea plantation, and those huge, lashing blue waves looked incredibly intimidating. The sea was like a lethal poison sapphire, drawing you towards it, though you always knew its touch would be deadly. But the water was just one of the challenges she would have to face if she was to escape the horrors of the last few years. Since Saker had kidnapped her, she had been drawn into his brutal world, pursued herself by the Clan, though she had done nothing wrong.

Now she was a fugitive, and though her first concern would always have to be anonymity, she still wanted to achieve something of worth with her days. This boat, and its mission to save the animals of the ocean, was perfect. For the first time in forever she felt happy, secure and optimistic. As long as she kept a low profile, all would be well. She certainly didn't want to be going overboard. A few weeks previously a colleague on a different ship had hit the waves and the mission had to be aborted while everyone else stopped to look for him. Sinter was determined that wouldn't happen to her; the new girl was not going to be the one holding everyone up . . . or drawing undue attention to herself.

The rest of her colleagues began making their last

minute safety checks, some strapping lifejackets over their oilskins, attaching themselves to the boat on safety lines. Others taped up cuffs and shoelaces; anything that could get caught once the hooks started flying. They were all well versed at this, hardcore activists from all over the world, who'd given up on their normal lives to be here on the front line, fighting for what they believed in.

Sinter took a deep breath and looked out at the Big Blue. It's sometimes said of the Pacific Ocean that it has no memory, which makes it the perfect place for a runaway, someone who wants to forget who they were and reinvent themselves in a world without horror. For a girl who'd spent the last two years of her life being chased around the globe by a band of faceless assassins, it was as close to home as she would ever get. There was no land in sight in any direction, just the endless dark blue, occasionally flashing tangerine in the last hints of sunrise. Soon it would be blazing hot, and she would have to cover every inch of herself or she would burn like a burger on a griddle.

"LINE!" the shout went up from her colleagues. Sinter threw back her hood, and saw the most spectacular sight of her life. A silver form erupted from the water, trailing diamond mist, its flanks flashing neon blue. The crescent-shaped tail drove it clear of the ocean, a long erect sail down its quicksilver spine. The rapier-like bill thrashed around in the air, seeking to impale an invisible attacker, as the sailfish – the fastest fish in the ocean – breached, seemingly in slow motion, before crashing down, creating an eruption of white lava. There was a unified gasp from the team. Nothing quite prepares you for seeing a sailfish breaching, a fish that can outswim a speedboat in short bursts, and seems to have been coated in titanium. But the sailfish would be too dangerous for them to try and release. That long sword of a bill could impale a potential rescuer, turning them into an unfortunate kebab. They were here to rescue other, less lethal, beasts.

"Dolphin!" shouted the captain, pointing behind the sailfish. Sinter followed the invisible line back from the white spume. The longline was being towed by a huge factory ship that would be many miles away, dragging both the longline and tens of thousands of fish-hooks attached to it. A curved dorsal fin broke the surface, then the dolphin rolled onto its side. There was a shriek from one of her colleagues as the huge hook flashed into view, protruding from the smiling beak of the dolphin. Then in unison another six or seven dorsal fins broke the surface, other members of the hooked dolphin's family, following their distressed sister, though there was nothing they could do to save her.

The speedboat came alongside the dolphin and accelerated to match its pace. The main longline was composed of tough metal and could not be cut. They would have to get to the hook itself to release the dolphin. Sinter's three colleagues made for the dolphin's side of the boat, and the strongest, a New Zealand Maori girl called Mistral, took up the catcher position, while a wiry Brazilian called Tomas grabbed her belt for security. This was the dangerous bit.

"Come to port," called Mistral. "PORT!"

The boat swung to the left, but slightly oversteered, and bumped the sleek grey form of the dolphin. She spooked and flinched from the boat's presence and dived with urgent flicks of her tail flukes.

"Careful!" yelled Tomas. "You're scaring her."

The captain cursed under his breath, and steadied the speedboat with one hand on the wheel, throwing stolen glances over his shoulder at the action.

The dolphin surfaced again, this time close. Sinter could see the long bottle-nosed snout that gives the species its name. Even now, in this fierce stress, she still seemed to be smiling, but a three hundred kilo dolphin with two hundred teeth is one of the most powerful predators on earth, and needs to be treated with enormous respect. Mistral grabbed out for the dorsal fin and, clasping it with one hand, thrust the other under the dolphin's belly. Instantly the animal began thrashing, screaming out its high-pitched stress calls. The other members of the pod surged in as close as they dared, calling out to their sister, terrified for her pain. The dolphin began twisting, slippery as a greased mackerel.

"I can't hold her," Mistral shouted. Tomas jumped in to help her, grabbing the dolphin. As Tomas lunged, the pair of pliers he'd been holding spilled from his hands, and slid across the deck. He turned to Sinter, face lashed with water and flecks of the dolphin's blood. "Get the hook!" he screamed.

Sinter dropped to her knees and fumbled for the pliers. They bounced in front of her as if the deck was a trampoline. The boat rolled sideways on the surge, propelling her to the guardrail, which thudded into her stomach, driving the air from her lungs. The sight beyond the guardrail stole her breath even more dramatically. Mistral and Tomas had the dolphin clasped in their arms, pressed close to the hull of the boat. Water sheened from its slick skin, which peels away every few hours to keep the animal streamlined.

The huge curved hook was as long as the giant meat-hooks she'd seen being used to hang beef carcasses when she'd been working in Saigon. And this hook had gone down into the gullet of the dolphin, before piercing out through its cheek. Blood ran freely down its flanks, its dark eyes stared at her in petrified terror, and then it let out a squeal like a human baby that cut Sinter through to her heart.

"Cut the barb!" winced Tomas. "You can do it!"

Sinter saw what he meant. The section of hook that protruded from the dolphin's mouth had a backwards-facing barb that prevented it from being removed.

"I can't hold her much longer." Mistral sounded exhausted.

Sinter fumbled with the pliers, then ripped off her gloves; she'd need more dexterity to deal with this. Leaning over the side of the boat, she pulled the long beak towards her. The first instinct was to stroke the terrified face, to try and convince the tortured mammal that everything would be fine, but time was short. Instead she clasped the hook with one hand and gripped the cutting scissor edges of the pliers around the barbed section of hook. Years on the run, all the physical training she'd done with her partner in crime Saker, months of lifting patients in foreign hospitals – all had hardened Sinter's sinews, but she'd never had to try and cut through solid metal on a bouncing boat before. She tensed her whole body, trying to focus her strength on her grip, but it was no use. She was tough, but not that tough. Their dolphin's struggles started to relax. Her next call was feeble; she was drawing her last gasps.

"We're losing her," Tomas gasped. "Do something!"

One of the other dolphins surfaced, nudging their sister. She looked up towards Sinter, eyes pleading. "Please don't let her die," he seemed to be saying.

At that second the world seemed to go into slow motion. Sinter saw a single drop of blood flying past her eyes. It was thicker, oilier than the water droplets that sailed alongside it. A wave towered high like a tumbling tower block, white streaks lining its length. The dolphin's dark pupil flickered towards Sinter, held her gaze. She started to recite a status report. "I can't generate sufficient force with one hand, so I need to switch to a double hand grip. As soon as I drop the hook with my other hand I lose control of the dolphin's beak. More than a second and she'll twist away from me. I need momentum, and it needs to be precise."

Riding the wave as it took them up, Sinter released her grip with one hand and grabbed the pliers with both. At that exact second, the boat rushed up to greet them, powering the blades together. Sinter centered all of her energy and force in that second in a *Kiaaii*, the ancient martial artist's yell of focus. There was a *chink* sound, the pliers spun from her hands, and the dolphin began thrashing again.

"You did it!" someone yelled.

The pliers had cut right through the metal barb. Sinter saw her chance, and grabbed for the hook again, twisting it out of the dolphin's mouth. It came free just as she convulsed with one critical lunge, wrenching herself free of her captor's grasp. Weighing as much as double fridge-freezer (though obviously far more graceful), the dolphin created a thunderous splash as she hit the water, and all three of them tumbled back into the boat.

They stood, shaking with effort and exhilaration. Behind them the pod of dolphins slowed and turned, surrounding their injured sister. As the crewmembers looked back, fighting to regain their breath, one lone dolphin leapt from the waves, somersaulting; then again, and again. It was a gesture of joy, of freedom, of relief, but to everyone on the boat it said just one thing: "Thank you."

Mistral turned to Sinter, her nut-brown features and

black eyes glowing with the effort and the thrill. A smile lit up her face. But before she could say anything, a low pitched *twang* rent the boat like a giant bass-guitar string. The metal longline sprang across the bows and hit Sinter squarely in the chest, tossing her across the boat. Mistral's face creased in disbelief, as huge hooks sliced across the decks in lethal curved shapes, whooping like loosed arrows. One pierced through her oilskin jacket. Her eyes widened and met Sinter's again. An eternity passed, that in reality was a millionth of a heartbeat, then the line caught tension, and Mistral was yanked off her feet and over the railings into the spray.

They saw the whites of her eyes and her clawing hands at the surface for a second, then she was dragged beneath the Blue.

2

Darkness began to lighten like a twisted dawn. Foggy reality began to focus into crystal clarity. There were sounds. Then voices. There were shadows. Then faces. It was like waking up from a sickening nightmare, not sure if you were still dreaming or entering another level of weird hallucinations. Saker had been through hideous awakenings like this many times, and knew that he just had to keep calm, and all would become clear. Raised in the Clan, he had been through more trials by torture than he cared to remember. Every time they looked for signs of weakness, the secret was to give nothing away until his head was clear.

A face loomed in close to his. It was human, and didn't have horns or an elephant's trunk. *Well that's something then*, Saker thought to himself. He blinked. There were two of them. Men. In army uniforms, carrying sticks . . . no, guns. AK47s. The uniforms were steel grey with red and white epaulettes. Saker flicked back through the ring binder files of his memory. *Ukranian*, he thought to himself. That would certainly fit with the language he could hear. He didn't speak any of it, but could recognise the speech patterns and sound. He made to reach for his top pocket to provide his ID, but couldn't seem to do it. His arms seemed too heavy. Then he realised: his hands were handcuffed behind his back. That would do it.

He shook his head, and blinked a few more times. The room was relatively small, but the walls were metal. And though his world was going round and round, it didn't have the tiny, barely perceptible but continual movements you get when airborne. He wasn't on the plane any more. His guess was that he was in a military installation, a soundproof and escape-proof interrogation room. A quick glance around the ceilings told him there were no obvious cameras, and no one-way mirrors either. And what of his captors?

They both sported shaved crewcuts, and they distinctly lacked necks; their collars revealing only bulldog-like neck rolls. Hefty, meaty hands with chipolata fingers gripped their weapons in an easy fashion that suggested they spent every day clasping them, and guns had long ago lost their novelty. They were grunts, but not to be taken for granted. Either of them could have finished him in minutes with a hand clasped over his mouth.

He shook his head; one of them was asking him a question.

"American?" he urged, in a fashion that showed he had been asking that same question for a while. Saker saw that his piggy eyes were blue as a whitewashed winter sky. The spongy flesh around his eyes was matched by a mishmash of scars at the brows and across the crook of a long-broken nose. A right bruiser.

"France? *Parlez-vous Français?*"

Saker shook his head.

"Ruski? Russian?" he almost spat.

His partner, who stood slightly behind him, stepped forward at this. It was a single step, but as he moved he shifted both hands on to the AK, raising it in readiness. A tiny move, but unmistakably threatening. Saker shook his head again.

"English? Do you speak English?"

Saker raised his face and made eye contact for the first time.

"Ah yes, you understand!" A hint of triumph in the man's voice. He turned to his silent friend and said something in his own language. Then back to Saker again.

"You causing big trouble for us, English, you know that? My friend here, he want to break you and drop your bones in the Black Sea!" At this he laughed heartily, but then abruptly stopped and slapped Saker in the face. "You hear me?" With that Saker's eyes flicked to the other guard.

"Why you look at him for? He's not going to help you! Nobody is coming to help you. In fact, just the other way."

With that he turned to his gun-bearing colleague and guffawed, the silent one smirking his agreement at their shared joke. Saker's ears pricked up at this.

"You understand that OK, eh?" Piggy grabbed Saker's face in one huge paw and squeezed his cheeks together. "Yes, someone is coming for you, little falcon boy. Someone I don't think you want to see."

Now it was the silent one's turn to speak. "What they say about this Prophet . . . they say he is some kind of butcher. When he have five minutes with you, you'll be screaming to have us back again. I'm pretty glad I'm not in that chair, falcon boy."

"The Prophet?" Saker had finally found words, but they didn't sound as if they'd come from his own mouth. "He's coming here?"

It was all Saker could do to repress the shudder that rattled up his spine. The Prophet was the commander of the Clan, a leader so quietly brutal that even the mention of his name had Clan boys cowering like beaten dogs. Since Saker had been on the run from the Clan, the Prophet had done all he could to silence him . . . permanently.

"It speaks! Show me money, Yevgeny!"

The previously sullen one, who was clearly Yevgeny, snorted and pulled a handful of crumpled notes from his pocket, handing one to piggy features.

"I bet him you speak in two minutes." He held up the note. "I win!"

Disgruntled, Yevgeny stepped forward again. "So what he want you for? You must have something pretty valuable he come here himself. What you got?"

Piggy looked keenly at Saker, with new interest. "You got something for me, falcon boy? Something nice?"

Saker met his eyes again.

"More valuable than a grunt like you'd understand."

Piggy shifted in his seat, and snort-giggled. Snorgled, perhaps. "Try me," he said, with icy resolve.

"Well I can't show you with my hands like this," Saker responded, yanking on his wrists to demonstrate the cuffs. At this they both laughed out loud.

"You think we just take those off you?" retorted Piggy. 'You really do think we're stupid.'

"Not really," said Saker. "There's two of you, you outweigh me, you're stronger than me." And then, matter-of-factly, he continued, "Oh, and you've got AK-Forty-sevens."

The two guards looked at each other. There was that.

Saker went on. "And if I don't have a chance of bargaining with you before the Prophet arrives here, then I am dead."

"What can you have to bargain with?" asked Yevgeny.

"Something that can change the world," Saker replied. "Something more valuable and important than you can even imagine."

"Oh really?" Piggy said. "And just where you keep these rich stuffs? We search you, you don't have nothing."

"You didn't search everywhere," Saker responded, then opened his mouth.

Piggy's eyes narrowed. He leaned forward, and cautiously peered into Saker's mouth, before letting out a little whistle. At the back of his mouth, tied neatly around one of his molars, was a thin white thread, which then proceeded down his gullet and into the abyss of his throat.

"What you got there, falcon boy?"

"I told you – take these cuffs off and I'll show you." Saker motioned to Yevgeny. "You keep your gun on me; I'm not going to try and fight you both."

There was a smirk again from Piggy, but it was half-hearted. He was unsure now. What should he do? They'd had no orders about what to do with the boy. As far as they knew he'd just had a panic attack on an airliner and had been Tasered. Piggy had no idea why they were taking it all so seriously anyway. What could it hurt? He was just a boy! His mind made up, Piggy took the keys from his belt and fumbled with Saker's handcuffs, springing them loose.

"Come then, let's see what treasure you got in your belly!"

Saker opened and closed his fingers, and felt the blood flowing back into his hands, massaging his wrists where the blue bruises would soon show. He was in no hurry. This magic trick would need to be delivered with a flourish, and he needed his fingers at their most nimble. Opening his mouth as wide as he could, he fished around his gums until he snagged the string. It was dental floss, thin enough to slide in between his teeth, strong enough not to break, and to be able to withstand the fierce corrosive power of his stomach acids. As he gently pulled on the thread, he gagged and felt the bile rise in the back of his throat. It was all he could do not to vomit.

"Hey, you don't puke on my carpet." It was half-hearted; Yevgeny was transfixed.

Saker started to pull the thread from his pursed lips, a conjurer unravelling silken lines of flags. He pulled for some seconds, until there was a clink: glass against the back of his tooth enamel. Opening his mouth, he revealed a glass vial bitten between his teeth. Both Piggy and Yevgeny leaned forward, as Saker revealed the treasure with a flourish between his fingertips.

"What is this?" Yevgeny asked in wonder.

Saker held his finger aloft to silence him. Yevgeny moved in alongside Piggy. Again, with the flourish of the magician, Saker held the vial aloft. It had perhaps a tablespoon of colourless fluid inside. He shook it from side to side. The liquid clung to the sides of the glass, and left a rainbow slick behind. Saker took the twist top in his fingers and opened the vial.

The guards fancied they heard a hiss, then the liquid evaporated and was gone. It was the most disappointing magic trick ever! They looked to Saker for an explanation.

"Have you heard of haemorrhagic fevers?" Saker asked. The guards looked at him blankly. "Airborne viruses. They travel from host to host like wildfire. Once you're infected, your brain starts to turn to mush, and you bleed to death. First from the inside, then from your eyes, your ears, your nose. There is no cure. Hanta virus, Red River fever . . . Ebola."

Piggy looked across at his colleague. The colour had drained from Yevgeny's face, and sweat was beading up on his forehead.

"What was in this vial was R-Forty-two haemorrhagic fever, a genetically modified virus, designed as a weapon by the Soviets. It makes Ebola look like a common cold."

Yevgeny had his hand clasped over his face. Piggy was starting to get the message as well. "But . . . but . . . you said you had treasure."

"There are unscrupulous people all over the world who would pay millions for this. It's the perfect weapon. Fast, utterly effective, totally incurable. What was in that vial was more powerful than an entire army, and could kill more people than a nuclear warhead."

"But you let it go? It's in the air?"

"Not any more," said Saker. "Now it's in your lungs, and making its way into your bloodstream."

"We have to get out!" Yevgeny was in full-on panic now, making for the door.

"I don't advise that." Saker was calm but firm. "This is the most virulent virus known to man. The second you open that door, it is airborne. Everyone on this base will be infected within minutes. It replicates inside your system and is passed on through the air you breathe out. And it breeds. It doubles in size every minute. The surrounding town will be infected in days, the region in weeks. Everyone you know will be as good as dead by the end of the week . . . if you open that door."

Yevgeny staggered back towards them, placing his rifle down on the desk as he went.

Piggy's eyes narrowed. "But you must be infected too . . . why you look so calm?"

"Well, it's simple," said Saker. "I know where the antidote is."

3

Despite having had the breath knocked out of her for a second time, Sinter didn't even break stride. She flung off her heavy oilskins and ran for the back of the boat, leaping once to make the bow rail, before propelling herself over the engines and into the Blue Beyond. As she hit the warm water, her boots weighed her down, so she shook them loose, and pulled herself with powerful strokes backwards through the water. The visibility was churned white by the whirring propellers, but once she was free of the bubbles, the glorious Blue opened out before her.

The salt stung her eyes, but even without goggles she could see pretty well. There it was – the writhing rusty brown longline snaking off into the distance. Sinter surfaced, sucking in air, determined to fill her lungs with as much oxygen as she could. With just seconds left, she breathed in with one desperate gasp and ducked back beneath the surface, reaching out with one hand. She grabbed the harsh metal line, and nearly had her arm ripped from its socket as it dragged her off into the flow.

Knowing she wouldn't be able to count on resurfacing to get another breath, Sinter gently allowed herself to slip back down the line, avoiding the clear plastic monofilament sidelines, which held the death trap of the fish-hooks. To get caught would be to be dragged to a certain drowning death. As she slipped down the line, she passed its deadly cargo, a glassy-eyed turtle long since drowned, then the bedraggled and lifeless form of an albatross.

These huge beautiful birds try and snatch the baited hooks from the surface and get dragged down to their doom. Many albatross species are now endangered thanks to these longlines, and as they mate for life, mates wait forlornly at the nest for a partner that will never return.

Sinter steeled her mind; she had to concentrate. And then she saw her, a lifeless form being hauled unceremoniously through the Blue. Sinter slipped just a little further until she could grab a hold of Mistral, all the while her lungs boiling and rasping with the effort of holding her breath.

It was too hard. She couldn't see, and couldn't hold her breath any longer. Clenching her eyes almost shut, she realised her underwater vision improved slightly. Now she could make out Mistral's form more clearly. She grabbed the line that linked the hook to the longline, and bit into it with all her force. But this was monofilament plastic line strong enough to restrain the world's most powerful fish; she had no chance.

Following it down, she found the hook passing through the shoulder and the hood of Mistral's oilskin. Frantically, Sinter started to rip at the zipper that was fastening the jacket. She'd been under too long! She needed to surface, but if she lost hold of the longline it was all over. Summoning all her strength, Sinter thrust the line above her head, and pointed her body down towards the seabed.

For just a second, the water hydroplaned down her body and propelled her upwards. She broke the surface for no more than a couple of seconds, but it was enough to grab another gulp of air before being wrenched down again. She had to succeed this time; she was tiring.

Concentrate, Sinter, she told herself. She took the zip in her fingers, and eased it downwards. Suddenly there was a yank, then a rush, and then stillness. She wasn't travelling with the longline any more. Mistral was in her arms, and they were free of the longline. Her orange oilskins bobbed off into the distance like laundry blown away in a hurricane. But now there was another problem. The Maori girl was powerfully built, heavier than Sinter and, without breath in her body, just wanted to sink like a lead weight.

Sinter didn't have enough puff to drag her to the surface. She needed more air. Sinter kicked and was in delicious air again, her body screaming for oxygen. She gulped it down desperately, hungrily, but knew time was not on her side. She had to dive again. Piking at the hips, she threw her feet skywards and dived again, finding the lifeless form of the girl not far below. Taking her under the shoulders, Sinter battled around to try and drag her up. But then, out of the corner of her eyes, she spotted something that turned her blood to ice.

A long, classic grey silhouette that has haunted every seagoing human's nightmares since we first began venturing out to sea. Sinter remembered the tales. The longlines are set to catch tuna and sailfish, but the greatest catch is sharks. Sharks that follow the sounds and vibrations of the clanking lines, and take vast bites out of the caught and vulnerable fish. Tiger sharks as long as minibuses; bull sharks that can bite through boats; mako sharks that travel almost as fast as the sailfish.

Her heart now thumping so loud she was sure the circling shark must be able to hear, Sinter surfaced with the lifeless girl. She had never felt so vulnerable in her entire life. Never felt quite so utterly exposed in an environment where she was totally unwelcome. The shark could take her in an instant, and no one would ever know. She wanted to scream, but she choked in her frantic desperation to draw breath, and to hold Mistral above the surface. Surely the boat would see them? Surely it would circle around and find them?

A fin broke the surface. A curved grey dorsal fin, which sliced through the water, dripping glossy sheen as it carved towards her. It's a cliché that your life flashes before your eyes in the moments before death, but it's true. Some scientists say it's because your brain is searching back through its past experiences, trying to find something that could help you out in your moment of peril.

What Sinter saw was a blaze of colour. She saw the plantation where she grew up. The beautiful mother she barely remembered, whose only image was emblazoned in a photo inside a locket she treasured more than her own life. She saw the moment her father had tried to bargain her away in an arranged marriage.

The flashbacks took her across her native India and into the Himalayas, into dungeons where she and Saker released captive tigers, and into jungles where they realised their calling and decided on their cause for the future. It took her up into the twirling snows of the Arctic, where together with Saker she had battled to stop hunters killing wolves. It took her right across the planet, but nothing she recalled was any use in this situation, in trying to avoid the three hundred scalpel-sharp teeth of a hungry predatory shark.

The fin was mere metres away. Sinter thrashed out at the water and yelled. She wasn't going down without a fight, not after all this! A startled beak broke the surface, and chattered at her. Sinter fought back her tears. Not a shark, but the smiling beak of a dolphin. Somehow, now she knew everything would be all right.

That was how the boat found them – Sinter frantically paddling to keep her friend afloat; the dolphin circling around them, keeping watch over them, guarding the pair as they were hauled aboard to safety.

A trickle of sweat formed at the end of Piggy's nose, formed itself into a neat ball, then dripped. The two guards clustered close to Saker, their eyes staring with fear. He had them right where he wanted them.

"There is an antidote, and I have it. But first of all I need a few answers of my own." He paused for dramatic effect. "I should remind you that the virus is already coursing through your bodies, attacking and killing cells. Soon those tiny virus particles will start to breed. Once they get to your brain, there is nothing I can do. Even the antidote won't help you. Time is not on your side."

Yevgeny and Piggy nodded eagerly to show that he should proceed.

"I need to know everything about where I am, how I got here, and who is coming to find me here."

The guards looked at each other. This was easy. They

both began at the same time, then Yevgeny stopped and nodded that Piggy should continue.

"It is very strange," he began. "You were on a plane, and you go crazy. They have to electrocute you for protection. For everybody protection," he clarified. Saker nodded. "But when the plane lands, usual you would just be given to police, not to us."

Yevgeny chipped in. "*Da*. We get call from our big boss, saying we have to bring you here. All very secret, like there is national security at stake. We don't understand, is just some crazy boy on a plane. No big deal."

He spread his hands and shrugged, with a gesture that showed *I guess we know why now!*

"But then we get you here, and we have instruction to hold you here until someone come for you."

"And where is here?" asked Saker.

"We are near Yalta." Yevgeny saw Saker didn't know the name. "It's nowhere, just a military camp on the Black Sea coast. That way," he pointed, "just mountains of Crimea. That way," he pointed in the other direction, then dropped his hand to indicate a big drop off, "is just a cliff and then the Black Sea. Is not big camp, but very secure."

Saker nodded that he should continue. "Then we get more call from the big boss. He say that someone very important will come for you. "The 'Prophet' he call him. Boss say this Prophet is some very bad guy. Like he is a spy or something."

Saker chewed on his lip. Was it possible? Would the Prophet come for him, in person? There had been so many mistakes in the past, perhaps he really did want to do it himself this time. Saker wondered for the umpteenth time quite how far the grasp of the Prophet and his shadowy Clan went. Saker had been brought up as Clan, trained and taught to identify with his totem animal, the saker falcon, to think and act like one.

In later years, along with other orphan boys, he was sent on secret and dangerous missions at the behest of the highest bidder. His predatory skills were used for evil purpose. Saker was the only boy who had escaped the talons of the Clan, and had been on the run ever since. Guilt had driven him to try and undo some of the damage he'd done, but though his conscience was now clear, he still couldn't shake his desperate need to find out where he'd really come from.

"How long?" Saker simply asked.

"Soon. Maybe just minutes."

He would need to act quickly.

"What about the antidote?" Piggy was desperate now. "I have a wife, a child . . . I cannot die like this."

Saker eyed them both, as if sizing them up. Then he reached down into his trousers and rummaged around. The two guards looked at each other with a mixture of amazement and horror. This boy really was full of surprises! Seconds later, Saker removed his hand, clearly concealing something about the same size and shape as the vial. He placed it on the arm of his chair and stood up, taking a few meditative paces.

Piggy reached over, his face wrinkled in disgust and, taking the object in a handkerchief, wiped it clean before holding it up in his fingers. The two of them looked at each other in confusion. "It's a bullet. A wooden bullet."

Yevgeny leaned in closer as he turned it around in his fingertips. It was indeed a wooden bullet, carved out of a tropical hardwood with exquisite grain. Turning it over to where the firing cap should be, he discovered the branded head of a falcon.

Yevgeny snatched it from him impatiently and tried to unscrew it to see if there was anything inside, but it was solid. "I don't understand . . ." he began, before turning around to look straight into the barrel of his own gun, this time in the hands of their young captive.

"That is the understatement of the century," said Saker.

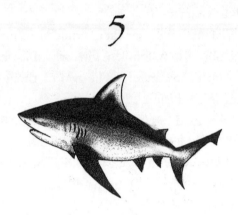

It took Mistral several days to get over her near drowning experience. For those days, the whole speedboat crew was confined to their main ship, no missions launched or risks taken. The *Galeocerdo* was merely the tender or support speedboat for their main floating home, a hulking, rusting old fishing trawler that had been converted to the cause. Crumbling red metal breaking through cracked paint, corroded by decades of salty air, it was a vessel that had clearly seen action. Below decks was a tangle of steaming pipes, chunking ancient machinery, creaking rivets and battered panels. It sometimes seemed a miracle the boat could float at all.

Named simply *Shark Saviour*, the trawler seemed to Sinter a little like a seaborne commune, staffed with earnest young people from all over the globe. Some were conservationists to the core, and just desperate to make a real difference. Others were lost, searching to find a purpose to their lives. They were a rag-tag bunch of eccentrics and fervent believers, fun and occasionally furious, unpredictable and interesting.

She sensed that a few were like her, on the run from dark secrets they wouldn't talk about. Apart from the captain, none of them had joined as competent seamen, but they had learned on the job, and now the boat bustled and buzzed with busy people, sometimes seeming to have far more than the twelve crew on board. Few used their real names. "Mistral" was just one marine word that had been taken on as a pseudonym. There was a "Wave", a "Coral", a "Zephyr" and a "Tempest".

Sinter pondered whether it was kind of like a new-age version of the Clan. As for her initial determination to avoid attention, that had completely gone out of the window after her heroic actions saving Mistral. The rest of the crew just didn't know how to treat her; she was clearly the youngest person on board, but had proven herself in a way few others would have dared. Some of the crew could barely contain their admiration; others were deliberately standoffish, intimidated by someone so capable and impressive, yet so young.

Every night they'd sit around eating whatever food could be concocted from the vegetable scraps they had left after weeks at sea. It was all vegan food, with lots of ingredients she'd never had before. However, after being given a stern talking-to by a posh-sounding English girl with dreadlocks called "Katabatic" about how eating meat was killing the planet through climate change, Sinter decided she'd rather eat tofu than be lectured.

"She's a rich kid with a massive chip on her shoulder," Mistral whispered conspiratorially. "Her dad's like a duke or something – she makes out as if she's a penniless lost soul, but every time we dock they've sent her a food parcel too big to get on board!"

Sinter smiled, but with a pang of sadness. There would be no parcels waiting for her when they made harbour. Not ever.

The *Shark Saviour*'s mission was to traverse the Pacific, searching for boats that were engaged in illegal fishing. Once they found them, they would hound them, doing all they could to throw a spanner in the works. The worst offenders were longliners, like the one that had so nearly claimed Mistral's life. These huge boats would trawl behind them longlines that could be sixty miles long, and the longlines would bristle with branch lines called ganglions, snoods or leaders. On those were tens of thousands of indiscriminate hooks. Though they were trying to hook tuna and sailfish, pretty much everything in the sea would be tempted by the baited hooks. The so called "bycatch" included whales, turtles and sharks. Hundreds of millions of sharks.

Though the circumstances were disheartening, and the conditions inside the rusting, airless hull unappealing, the boat was nevertheless a jolly place. Everyone took turns cooking, trying desperately to find a new take on beans, greens and peanut butter. After dinner they would all sit around while someone strummed a guitar, or play cards and share travelling stories about places they'd been and things they'd seen. One evening an Irish lad started talking about how much he wanted to go to the Arctic, and she realised she knew the place he was talking about.

"I know the Yamal," she blurted out. "I used to work there."

"In Siberia?" The Irish boy was stunned. "You worked in Siberia?"

It seemed the whole room hushed. Sinter blushed deep. "I . . . yeah, I just herded reindeer. Just kept away the wolves. Just . . . just . . ."

"You kept away the wolves?" The Irish boy sounded as if she had claimed to be the first woman to set foot on Mars.

"But I thought you said you'd been a nurse?" the posh English girl demanded incredulously. "How old are you anyway?"

Sinter stuttered into silence. She felt the whole room staring at her secrets.

"That doesn't matter." Mistral stepped in firmly. "No past, no history, only the future, remember? Sinter's business is her own."

Sinter breathed a deep sigh. Mistral was a good ally. It was a shame she hadn't consulted her on a name change. Everyone knew her as Sinter now, so there wasn't much point in coming up with something new.

*

Confined to the decks of the main ship, Sinter needed a project to keep her busy. Having struggled to hold her breath for long enough to save Mistral in the whole fish-hook episode, she decided to find out if she could get better at it. Her help came in the form of the very person she'd saved.

Mistral, it turned out, had been a yoga teacher before joining the boat. That fit perfectly. With her tousled black hair and eyes and her muscular shoulders and arms, she looked like someone who trained hard. No one would have called her conventionally pretty, but there was something about her that was undeniably attractive: an air of mischief in the sparkling eyes and slightly upturned nose. And she had a certain aura about her, wisdom beyond her years, a sense that she knew stuff, that she had the secret of life and happiness. She seemed like someone who would be calm in a crisis, and useful in a battle.

Sinter had trusted and liked her instantly. Perhaps best of all though, Mistral had studied how to control and become more efficient at breathing, a central tenet of yoga, but also of freediving. From dawn, they'd sit up on deck, stretching and relaxing, bringing their heart rates down as low as they possibly could.

"The thing about holding your breath for a long time," Mistral said, "is that it's not about how big a breath you can take. Whales and seals actually breathe out before they dive. It's not about the air in your lungs, it's about the air in your blood and muscles. If you can relax, and breathe deeply for long enough beforehand, then your whole body becomes your scuba tank."

The two of them would practise for hours, doing all kinds of breathing exercises, before challenging each other to see who could hold their breath for the longest. To begin with, Sinter really struggled, and would give in to the temptation to breathe after only a minute or so. But after just a few days, she was getting better and better.

"You know there are Bajau sea gypsies in Indonesia who can hold their breath for seven or eight minutes like this," Mistral told her. "They walk along the sea bed catching fish and collecting shells. It's incredible what you can achieve with training."

The ship was travelling through the very waters where the Bajau roamed, a tropical sea peppered with islands. Some of the islands were perfect volcanic cones, rising steeply out of the water, dark and brooding, often still smouldering with plumes of smoke. Others were once coral reefs, but had been lifted up over deep time by the trundling movements of the shifting tectonic plates. Both types were blessed with lush green forests, leaning palm trees and fine sand beaches. Some had pure white sands, but the volcanic islands had shiny black sands that were too hot to walk on.

At the end of a week confined to ship, the boat dropped

anchor in a sheltered inlet. As they cruised in closer to land, the water became quickly shallower, changed from deep blue to aquamarine and then became so clear that, visible beneath the surface, were the extravagant shapes of a coral reef. Or what had once been a coral reef. Now below the surface was just a jumble of bleached white branches of dead coral.

"Bombing scumbags," the captain muttered.

"They chuck dynamite into the reef," he explained, "and when it blows up, the fish all float to the surface. Or sometimes they pump cyanide into it. It's a poison. Kills the fish, and kills the coral. It'll never grow back, but they don't care. It's all about the quick buck. No one thinks about the future."

Towards the edge of the white coral was a steep drop off, where the sea fell away from wading depth into seriously deep water. While the captain and crew took photographs, and logged the damage to the coral, Mistral and Sinter took a mask and snorkel and swam over the destruction. On a shallow sand shelf, Sinter saw a pretty-looking shell, shaped like an ice-cream cone, with beautiful speckles all over it. She ducked under and reached out for it, but was grabbed by her friend.

"That's a cone shell!" Mistral scolded. Sinter looked at her, not comprehending. "A cone shell – the most venomous snail on earth!"

Mistral sighed and rolled her eyes as if to say, "You don't know anything," then beckoned to show that Sinter should follow her underwater. As Sinter looked, Mistral pointed out the billowing skirts of the snail beneath the shell; it was alive!

She pointed to the tube that stuck out of the narrow end of the cone, and wagged her finger. Then Mistral picked the shell up by the fat end and brought it up to the surface.

"So the thick end of the cone is fine," she explained, "but the thin end has a bit that can extend out the front and envelop a fish. Then a tiny little harpoon fires out and kills the fish."

"But why would it stab me? I'm too big for it to eat."

"Well yeah," her friend answered, "usually what happens is someone sees a pretty shell, picks it up and puts it in their pocket. Then, as it's bouncing around, the cone shell gets all upset and fires off. Into their leg. People have died from these things, you know."

Sinter looked with new respect at the strange snail in front of her. The reef was certainly full of surprises.

"Pretty much everything down here is toxic," Mistral added, "which is why it's usually best to look, but not touch!"

It was the perfect place to practise their new freediving skills. Sinter hung at the surface, breathing as deeply as she could, concentrating on blowing out bad air, and saturating her tissues with good, oxygenated air. She relaxed as much as she could, feeling her heartbeat dropping, the so-called "mammalian dive reflex" that allows seals and whales to explore the depths for, in some cases, more than an hour at a time.

Finally, when she felt the time was right, she looked over to her friend, gave her the OK symbol, and they both tumbled in the water and swam down, out over the drop off. As they cruised over the edge, the depth that suddenly appeared below was dizzying, like vertigo. It was as if she had just flown over a cliff edge, and felt the world drop away beneath her feet.

As they dropped along the wall, they glided down into a world of colour Sinter had never seen before. The corals were arranged like flower gardens, with electric blue and yellow fish flitting like butterflies and birds between the plants.

Already she was fighting the overpowering urge to breathe and reminding herself to relax and enjoy the spectacle unfolding before her. All the creatures were new to her, apart from a few fish she may have enjoyed on a barbecue once upon a time. But then Sinter started. She saw a familiar and sinister silhouette out of the corner of her eye, and this time it really wasn't a dolphin.

Shark! She made to bolt for the surface in panic, but found she couldn't move. Something had a hold of her hand. She looked around to see that her friend had taken her palm in hers, and Mistral was smiling.

"Relax," she seemed to be saying, "enjoy it."

Sinter turned back. The shark was slightly longer than she was, grey above and white below. And far from hurtling towards them to savage her, the shark seemed to be cruising along minding its own business, showing them no interest whatsoever. Within seconds, Sinter's terror turned to fascination. The shark was so sleek, so effortless underwater; languid sweeps of its tail were enough to keep it cruising along, clearly not in hunting mode.

The glorious, elegant fish swept alongside her, and Sinter extended her hand towards its flank. As the shark swam away from her, the skin was as silky as that of the dolphin. But when she brushed her hand the other way, she gasped in surprise. In the other direction the skin was as harsh as sandpaper.

Tiny burs on the shark's skin create micro-turbulence as water flows over it, making the water almost greasy, lubricating the shark's path through the Blue. Olympic swimmers had copied this sharkskin in their full body swimsuits, until it was deemed to give them an unfair advantage and they were banned.

The shark twitched slightly to the side, almost as if it had enjoyed her touch. It made as if to swim away, then thought better of it, and turned back on itself so its snout was aiming straight for Sinter. Her eyes widened, but Mistral still had a hold of her hand. Fighting every sinew in her body telling her to swim as fast as she could away from this monster, Sinter reached out again, and let her fingertips caress the snout of the shark. It felt rough to the touch. The shark gaped its fearsome mouth, showing off its vicious-looking teeth, but it didn't bite. Instead, it stopped swimming and hung in the water, nudging her hand with its nose. It was as if it was an enthusiastic puppy dog demanding to be stroked.

Astounded, Sinter gave the fish what it seemed to want, rubbing its snout gingerly. She looked on in wonder as the shark's eyes seemed to roll back into his head and it convulsed sideways as if in some kind of ecstasy.

She couldn't have known it, but sharks have ultra-effective organs in their snouts, which pick up on the weak electrical fields created inside the moving muscles of their prey. They are so incredibly sensitive that stimulating them like this pretty much overwhelms the shark, and they fall into a trance. Without knowing what she was doing, Sinter had hypnotised a shark!

The incredible experience had distracted Sinter from the burning in her lungs, but she knew that now she simply had to breathe or she was in trouble. Tugging on Mistral's hand, she pointed to the surface. Her friend nodded, and they started upwards. Sinter was astounded at how far they had descended and at how far above them the surface appeared, a shimmering mirror that seemed an eternity away.

Seconds later, though, they burst through the glass and gulped in sweet air. Sinter suddenly felt vulnerable again at the surface. As soon as she had caught her breath, she plunged her face back in to look down below her, but the shark was nowhere to be seen.

6

The hollow hole of the gun barrel was pointing straight in between his eyes. *I could have cleaned it a bit better this morning*, Yevgeny mused to himself.

"What is this?" Piggy demanded. He was trying to sound commanding, but his mastery had left him long ago.

"This," Saker replied, "is what's known in the con artist's game as a Kansas City Shuffle. Sleight of hand, smoke and mirrors, designed to get you both to take your eyes off the ball for just a second." He proffered the gun. "That was all I needed."

"So you mean there is no antidote?" Yevgeny sounded utterly wretched, suddenly seeing his life crumbling, his days coming to an end, vomiting blood surrounded by faceless people in huge Hazmat suits. A groan shook him from his visions. His companion had his porcine face in between his sausage fingers.

"No, you idiot," Piggy eventually intoned. "He means

there is no virus. No Ebola, no damn RT-Twenty-four or whatever. He conned us."

"But the vial?" stuttered Yevgeny. "You had the toxin in the vial, you swallowed it . . ."

"No, he just had to make us believe he did. And we did." Piggy looked up at Saker with new respect. "You plan this whole thing? Everything?"

Saker snorgled. "Not everything. The getting Tasered bit I could definitely have done without. But the rest – well, most of it – yes, I planned it."

Yevgeny shook his head. "But why? You didn't need to do any of this. Why you need to escape from here? If you hadn't gone crazy you wouldn't be here? And now this Prophet is coming to find you. It doesn't make any sense."

"I *want* the Prophet to come here," Saker said. "That's the point. I've been wanting to meet him like this for a long time." And then, lifting the gun in his hand like a trophy, he continued, "When I have the upper hand."

At that moment, the phone on the desk rang, and all three of them jumped out of their skins. They stared at it, speechless, not knowing what to do. Piggy looked up at Saker. "What you want me to do? I answer it?"

"No need," said Saker. "That's him, he's on his way. And I'll be waiting."

The three stood in tensed silence, staring at the ringing phone. Saker flexed his fingers around the stock of his gun. It stopped.

"So what we do now?" Piggy asked.

Saker bit his bottom lip and assessed his options. A plan began to hatch in the back of his brain. "OK, so you take these," he said, taking the handcuffs he had just been released from, and throwing them to Yevgeny, "and put them on your friend here."

Yevgeny went to tie Piggy's hands behind him, but Saker stopped him. "No, put his hands in front of his body."

Next he took Yevgeny's own cuffs from his belt, and restrained the other Ukrainian in the exact same way. "Now I want you both to stand with your backs to the door, and you, you hold this." With that, he took the other AK47, popped out the magazine, emptied it of bullets, then returned it and gave it back to Yevgeny.

Then Saker dragged the chair he had been restrained in until it was facing the door and sat himself down, with his hands behind his back and the rifle resting across his palms, below the seat of the chair. It was far from invisible, but would probably not be seen on a first, fleeting inspection. Now all they had to do was wait.

The minutes ticked away like hours, Saker's mind scampering through every eventuality; through his course of action once that door opened. What would he say when he was finally faced with the man who had been his torturer? The man who had trained him to be a thief, a poacher, a criminal, an assassin? The man who had stolen his childhood and his past, and then pursued him across the world, swearing to kill him and destroy any evidence that he had ever lived? The man who had tried to turn

Sinter into a Clan member too, and had tried to brainwash her so she would slit Saker's own throat.

Saker's hatred boiled inside of him like acid. How could he hold back from just squeezing the trigger, and wiping the slate clean? How much better off would the world be without the sinister and secret power of the Prophet and the Clan? But no. There were too many questions to be asked. Saker needed to know. Where did he come from? Who was he? Did he have a family? And . . . was there something in there he would rather not know?

The questions, conundrums and doubts that swirled around in his mind were broken as the door handle turned and the metal door creaked open. This was the moment he'd waited a lifetime for.

Then he gasped, drawing in a short, sharp intake of breath. A familiar shape seemed to glide into the room, with an impossibly light footfall, its broad, muscular torso appearing to float free above a Lupine lower body.

7

That evening, back on the ship, the two of them sat on deck, watching the sun set while the others squabbled and ate below decks.

"I don't understand," Sinter said eventually. "Why didn't it eat us? Surely it could have eaten us if it wanted to?"

"Of course," replied Mistral, "but the fact is they just don't."

"Well . . ." Sinter was choosing her words carefully, trying not to sound stupid. "Why didn't he?"

"That kind of shark only feeds on other fish," Mistral replied. "They've been around for over four hundred million years, and are very good at working out what's good for them to eat and what isn't."

Sinter frowned. "OK, but what if it was a different kind of shark? Or if it was in a bad mood? Or, really hungry?"

"Sharks can go months without food," said Mistral,

"and they just don't attack people. Of course there are a few people killed by sharks in a year, and they make big headlines, but that's one or two people, in our planet of seven billion! Loads of things kill one or two people a year. Falling coconuts kill more than that!"

Sinter sniggered.

"It's not a joke, it's true," Mistral continued. "Falling soft drinks machines kill more people than sharks, and you're hundreds of times more likely to be killed by a bolt of lightning than by a shark. Last year more people were killed by selfies than by sharks. Honestly, they're one of the least dangerous animals to us human beings. We just psych out because they look so scary. And the media and movies and stuff."

Sinter looked long and hard at the Maori girl to see if she was serious. "All right, let's say I believe you. That's all fair enough, and I have to admit that was really cool down there today. But why are you so worried about sharks, then? I mean, why more than the dolphins and the turtles and the whales and everything else? What's so special about them?"

Mistral examined the young Indian girl intently, and then spoke. "There's something you need to see."

Every few weeks, *Shark Saviour* would pull ashore to get fresh supplies, and also to give the crew a chance to stretch their legs and prevent them from going stir crazy. The captain had to be quite careful about which islands and towns he chose to land at, as some of them were completely dominated by the fishing industry and knew *Shark Saviour* by reputation. He told stories of the boat being forced to pack up quickly and leave harbour before a local mob arrived to try and sink them.

The sleepy island they pulled in at this time didn't seem to mind though. Like many Western Pacific islands, it was little more than a green lump in the sea, with swaying palm trees and a ramshackle village by the harbour, composed of brightly painted but fading wooden houses. Chickens and pigs snuffled about the dusty streets.

Most of the crew made for the local market, where they bought all the fresh fruit and vegetables they could find, bartering for a good price with the local sellers. Mistral and Sinter headed along the coast, away from the main village. As they walked, Mistral began to tell Sinter a little of her life back home in New Zealand.

"I'm from a small town in the South Island," she said, "not much to set it apart from the rest of the country really. But in New Zealand you're never far from the ocean, and it's natural to grow up caring for it."

She told Sinter that her dad had been a fisherman, and had gone out every day using a rod and line to catch fish, which he would then sell in the market. But it got harder and harder for her father to catch the fish he needed. He started to complain about "thieving factory ships" from foreign countries coming in and stripping the sea of everything, taking all the fish he used to catch and leaving nothing for the local fishermen. Eventually there was nothing left to catch. Her father had to give up fishing and take a different job, but he was a broken man. He never got over losing the family business.

As Mistral and Sinter walked, they passed small wooden kiosks on wheels selling coconut water and sweet snacks. The sellers rested in the shade of spindly palm trees, smoking cigarettes with a powerful spicy smell of cloves, watching the world go by. Rounding a headland, the two girls looked down to a beautiful bay, peppered with other green islands sprouting from the turquoise waters. The vista was somewhat tempered by a warm blast of overpowering odour.

"Wow, what is that?" Sinter gasped, wrinkling her nose.

"That's what I've brought you here to see," Mistral responded.

Over the brow of the next hill, the pair were rewarded with a bizarre sight. For hundreds of metres there were wooden racks like huge trestle tables, covered with grey triangles that were bleaching and drying in the fierce tropical sun. The tables stretched off as far as the eye could see, and every square centimetre was covered with the fish-smelling triangles. Several brooding dark-haired men watched the girls with suspicion, fingering the battered-looking machine guns that hung around their necks.

Sinter stepped forward and took one of the triangles in her hands. There was something deeply familiar about it.

"What are they?" she asked.

"Shark fins," Mistral responded.

"Fins?" Sinter was incredulous, and saw in her mind's eye the beautiful, silvery flanks of the shark she'd so recently seen for real, alive. "But . . . each shark only has one dorsal fin . . ." She looked off into the distance at the stacks and stacks of fins, and tried to do calculations in her head. "There must be fins from *thousands* of sharks here."

"Tens of thousands," Mistral corrected. "And this is just one day, in one week, on one small island, in one country of the world."

Sinter frowned, and tried to comprehend the enormity of what she was being told. "But that doesn't make any sense." Looking down at the springy, rotting piece of flesh in her hand, she asked, "Surely no one would eat this?"

"Well, not like that," Mistral responded, "but it's a tradition to boil it up and make a soup out of it. Shark-fin soup. It's really popular at weddings in China, Vietnam, Taiwan, places like that."

"So what happens to the rest of the shark?" Sinter asked.

"Well, the fin is the bit that's worth the money, the rest of the shark is pretty much worthless, so they just throw it back."

"They throw it back?" Sinter was appalled. "Without its fins? How does it swim?"

"It doesn't," replied Mistral. "It sinks and it dies." She

stopped and drew a long breath. "At least a hundred million sharks every single year."

As they walked the length of the trestle tables, allowing the enormity of the situation to sink in, Sinter noticed one of the guards moving towards them, fingering the trigger on his rifle. He had faded blue tattoos running down his forearms and a spindly moustache – and he looked like trouble.

"We should probably make ourselves scarce," Mistral said. She'd noticed the guards too. "These fins are worth so much money that they guard them pretty closely."

"So what do we do?" Sinter asked. "This can't go on! There'll be no sharks left."

Mistral sighed, and looked to the ground. "Who knows?" She gestured out towards the open ocean. "Out there is just a free for all right now – no rules, no government, no protection. If we don't do something, no one else will."

Sinter nodded. By now the guard had covered the distance to the pair of them and stood right in their faces with a threatening manner.

"No picture," the guard said. "No photo. This private."

They held up their hands to show the approaching guard they meant no harm and weren't going to take any incriminating photos, then turned and walked back off down the hill the way they'd come.

They walked in a heavy silence, both glum with the implications of what they'd seen. Sinter's mind was racing.

She needed a new cause, a focus. After all, she had money. There was still a small fortune left over from their successful sting of a Malaysian logging baron, conning him out of cash he had himself stolen. All that money was sitting gathering more money in a secret bank account. And she still maintained her contact with Minh, her Vietnamese acquaintance who had an uncanny ability with the dark world of internet espionage and was part of a network of lawless hackers connected across the globe. There was great potential there and responsibility, too. If there was something she could do, then she simply had to do it. But first she would need to make contact with Saker, and start to shape a plan.

At that thought, her frown deepened. Saker was her most powerful ally and the only person on earth who knew her story. He had been through so much with her. But he had his own demons to battle, and clearly had other things on his mind. When they parted, it had not been on good terms; Sinter had been desperately trying to get through to the good she knew must be buried somewhere under all the hate, but Saker was so obsessed with his quest for answers and vengeance that he barely seemed to register her existence.

Who knew where he was now, and what trouble he was in?

8

Their eyes met for the first time in many months. The dark, sharp eyes of a falcon against the piercing golden pupils of the foe who was once his mentor and leader.

"Hello, Saker."

Their gaze held, as if they were trying to stare each other down, and the breath caught in the back of his throat. Saker's heart plunged into his guts.

"Hello, Wolf," he replied.

This he hadn't planned for. All the effort, all the forward thinking, it had all been about orchestrating a confrontation with the Prophet, one in which he held all the cards and had his tormentor totally at his mercy. After all the disastrous attempts of Clan members to capture Saker, he had thought that the Prophet would come himself this time. But instead he had sent Wolf. The Clan member who had once been his brother, but now hated him more than any other. There was no formal system of seniority or ranking in the Clan, but Wolf had always been a leader. Since Saker had been a fugitive, he had become the thorn in Wolf's heel. Wolf's hatred had become all-consuming.

"Looks as if your days of running are finally finished," Wolf began. "I'll be taking you back with me."

"After the way you messed up the last few times, I was expecting the Prophet to come himself," Saker snarled, "rather than sending his *lap dog*."

Wolf baulked slightly at this, but soon recovered his composure. "I have been given a last chance." He fixed Saker with a challenging stare. "No failures will be accepted this time. If you try and escape, I have permission to execute you immediately."

With that he lifted the front of his tunic to reveal a scabbard with a long dagger tucked into the front of his trousers.

"Wow," Saker replied, sounding unimpressed. "I'm a little disappointed, if I'm honest. I expected rather more of a welcoming party. And certainly more hardware. Particularly as I've got this."

With that, he swung the AK47 from under his chair and effortlessly into a firing stance, the barrel levelled at Wolf's chest.

"Unless, of course, you've got an awful lot better at throwing that knife since I saw you last."

There was a certain amount of performance about

Saker's unveiling of the rifle, and the reaction was exactly what he had hoped for. Wolf's jaw dropped open, and he blinked several times as if he couldn't believe what he was seeing and was trying to use his eyelids as windshield wipers to clear his vision. Wolf then turned towards the two guards, and saw for the first time that their hands were cuffed together. Piggy shrugged at him in an embarrassed manner. "You might as well shoot me now," Wolf said. "The Prophet made it clear what would happen if I messed up again."

Wolf's voice faltered slightly as he remembered the moment that his master had taken him to a clearing in an ancient forest, and told him that all the Clan boys who had failed or rebelled were buried there beneath the grass. It was a clear threat as to the fate that awaited Wolf, too, if he should disobey.

"Well, we'll get to that in a bit," said Saker, "but first I need some answers."

He now sat facing Wolf.

"You," he ordered Piggy, "take his knife out and throw it over in the corner."

Piggy did as he was asked.

"And put those extra cuffs on him too."

Then Saker addressed the handcuffed Wolf. "Now, tell me where I can find the Prophet."

Their conversation lasted no more than ten minutes. That was all it took for Saker to bleed Wolf of all his information, and to exhaust all his questions.

Finally, they sat in silence, two mortal enemies, their battle finally done.

"So what happens now?" asked Wolf. "You'll never outrun us, Saker. You're just delaying the inevitable. Are you planning on just waltzing out of here and causing chaos?"

Saker was quiet, clearly lost in thought. Then he replied, "Pretty much. You two," he barked towards the guards, "I'm guessing you'd like to come out of this smelling sweet, rather than having been outsmarted by a teenager."

The sorry-looking pair examined each other. Their gaze said that sounded just great to them.

"You were given charge of one foreign boy with this hair," he pointed to both his shaven haircut, and then to Wolf's identical head. "Someone of our age, our height, our build, our faces."

The guards looked them over. It was true – the pair of them were near identical, apart from their eye colour.

"So I'm going to walk out of here, and you're going to keep him instead," he said, pointing to Wolf now. "No one will be any the wiser."

The three of them looked at him as if he'd just emerged from an asylum, clad in a straitjacket and singing lullabies to himself.

"But when the boss man find out," Yevgeny began, "when this boy do not return with you, then boss will go mad, and then we . . ." With that he made the noise for someone's throat being cut (though he couldn't make the movements with his hands cuffed).

"I don't think so," Saker replied. "As Wolf here has already said, this was his last chance. He messed up one too many times. No one's coming to get him. We have no real identities, no history, no caring parents wanting to find us. Just put my documents on him, slam him up in prison and throw away the key."

The three of them all appeared to ponder this in slack-jawed silence, thinking through whether the simple but audacious plan would work.

"It'll never work," Wolf scoffed. "The Prophet would never just leave me here." He didn't sound as if he believed his own words.

"Maybe not," reasoned Saker, "but as you said, you've had your last strike. Either he'll leave you here to rot in my place, or he'll send someone in here to silence you permanently."

He turned to the guards. "And if you two are really worried, perhaps he could be a victim of an escape attempt gone wrong."

With that the guards looked knowingly at each other. That would certainly be a neater ending to the whole mess.

"Either way, you keep your mouths shut, and nobody ever needs to know you had your guns taken and your bottoms spanked by a kid with a wooden bullet and some dental floss!"

Wolf looked at the three newly-made accomplices in

astonishment. He could see they'd already made up their minds. The awfulness of his predicament hit him full on.

"Saker," his voice was now wavering, pleading, "please. I'm begging you. We grew up together, we're Clan. You know me – I need to be free. You can't leave me in a cage . . . that would be worse than dying. Please, just shoot me now and get it over with."

Saker had a vision of Wolf in a prison, pacing up and down in ceaseless torment, just like his wild namesake does when kept in a cage. He meant it; he would rather Saker just execute him, a clean death, honour amongst thieves.

Saker raised the gun and shifted his grip. It really was the most humane thing to do. Wolf gritted his teeth and clenched his jaw, ready for the explosion of sound.

Saker relaxed his fingers on the stock of the gun. A burst of gunfire in this confined, metal-walled place would not be wise. Plus the sound might well bring other guards running. Wolf didn't deserve that much compassion. Instead, Saker rifled through the pockets of his restrained enemy, finding a passport, a wallet crammed with cash of several different currencies, a smartphone and a small torch. Saker took them all. He then snapped the temporary ID badge off Wolf's tunic and clipped it onto his own. He took the keys for the guard's handcuffs and tossed them over into the corner.

"Give it ten minutes before you unlock yourselves," Saker said. "You can do it quicker if you want – you can sound the alarm if you feel like it – but just remember, unless I walk out of here a free man, and he goes behind bars . . ." he paused for dramatic effect, "then you two are going to take the blame for all of this. Your call."

"Saker brother, I'm begging you," Wolf pleaded. "As one predator to another – don't leave me here like this."

Saker looked back at him. "Sooner or later we all have to pay for our crimes, Wolf."

With that, he walked out of the door. He propped up the gun, composed himself, and started down the corridor ahead of him.

For the first time in years, he knew exactly where he was going.

9

The captain stood on the bridge of the *Shark Saviour* in darkness, eyes flickering about between the few modern instruments, the charts, and the silver moon reflecting and dancing on the black sea beyond. Night on the *Saviour* was generally spent anchored in port, safe from unseen sunken rocks and small fishing boats. It was unusual for them to be under steam right through the night.

Sinter stepped up onto the bridge with caution. She'd only been up here a few times in daylight and had no idea what the protocol was. The captain started as he sensed her approach.

"I'm sorry, Captain," Sinter said. "I didn't mean to startle you. Brought you some noodles."

He nodded to the counter beside him, indicating that she should put it there.

"And a smoothie," she added. "It has a whole bunch

of veggies I've never seen before in it. Plus some apple and ginger. It kind of looks like pond slime, but it tastes OK."

The captain smiled, and gestured that she could come up and stand alongside him at the wheel.

"It's quite something, isn't it?" he said. "The sea by night."

Sinter nodded her agreement. The water looked like black velvet, or a slick of endless dark oil, sheened with glorious, white, shimmering light. It was hypnotic.

"Why are we steaming through the night, Captain?" she asked.

"The *Moumoko Maru* has continued travelling west, so we need to follow," the captain answered. In the moonlight the wrinkles of his face seemed like bottomless trenches, but silver glinted in his eyes. "There are several big national marine parks there, including Komodo."

"Komodo?" questioned Sinter with interest. "Where the dragons live?"

"Yup, but it's also one of the finest underwater marine reserves on the planet. If the *Maru* trawls her lines and nets through there it would take a decade to recover."

Sinter understood. The risks of journeying at night were outweighed by the threat to the ocean life.

The *Shark Saviour* had been trailing one particular fleet for near two months now, doing their best to approach with stealth and then pounce with precision. The boat they had fastened on to was called the *Moumoku Maru*, out of Shanghai. It was truly colossal – twenty thousand tonnes, making it as heavy as fifty jumbo jets – and was on a three-month journey, tearing its deadly trail around the islands of Indonesia and the Philippines, sticking to the less inhabited waters where there was no law.

The *Shark Saviour* and the *Maru* had been engaged in a lethal dance, the *Saviour* sending raids to release the catch, and to try and snare the larger boat. The *Maru* had plenty of ways to defend themselves though, and they were not constrained by morality. The *Maru* was part of an armada of vessels from the largest fishing countries, like Spain, Japan, Taiwan and China, which were far, far from home, supposedly operating in international waters.

However, around every country with a coastline, there extend waters that belong to that nation. Waters where these factory ships are never supposed to catch fish. All countries have limits and laws about how you take fish in their waters. If you take too many young or small fish that haven't yet had the chance to breed, then a few years later you don't get any fish at all. If you take excessive catches of endangered fish like Pacific tuna, then there is simply no way that animal is going to survive extinction. If you take all of one kind of predator like sharks, then the balance of the ecosystem falls apart and bad things start to happen.

Most countries have marine sanctuaries, places where fishing is completely illegal, to allow fish and other wildlife to recover. Unfortunately these sanctuaries then end up being the very best place to fish. So the factory fleets run illegal catching trips into these parks, particularly in the coastal seas of less wealthy nations that don't have the security forces to repel them. They simply take everything they can, without limit. It is a tragedy.

Knowing all this, when *Shark Saviour* picked up one of these destructive machines, they wouldn't let it go, keeping on their trail like a bloodhound.

"When future generations look back on our times," the captain told Sinter, with great sadness in his voice, "they will see this as our biggest crime."

Sinter thought of all the terrible things she'd seen in the years since she had been free, and nodded solemnly.

"You'd think we'd have learned by now. We know how much of nature we need to protect in order for our world to work. We know what the consequences will be if we take and destroy everything from our seas and our forests . . . and yet we do it anyway," she said.

The captain nodded and, when he turned to her, she saw he had a tear glistening in the corner of one eye. "Yes. I see so much beauty out here on the High Seas: the mobula rays that leap from the water as high as a man, the white orca that hunts the volcanoes of the Aleutians, white bears walking across icebergs the size of cities, the blue whales that are bigger than my boat and have a spout that can drench us all in its spray. I am a lucky man to have seen such marvels. I fear your children may never see these things."

To see such emotion from the gnarled old sea dog made

Sinter's heart skip, and she reached out and took the captain's hand in hers.

"You don't really think we'll lose these things do you, Captain?" she asked.

He looked at her sorrowfully. "I've been around a lot longer than you, and I just don't have any faith left in people. People would cut down the last giant redwood tree to make a coffee table. They'd slaughter the last dolphin if it meant a few dollars, mine the mountains so they could have a better television."

"We won't let them win," Sinter insisted. "As long as people have hope. As long as people like us carry on making a difference, knowing that there is something we can do. One person alone *can* change the world. They just need to believe they can."

The captain studied his young crewmate with newfound respect. "Thank you," he said. "Sometimes it's easy for an old man like me to lose the way. I see so much horror." Wiping his eyes with his sleeve, he went on, "It's time for me to find the light again."

At that moment, there was a hideous tearing noise and a sickening jolt, stopping the boat and throwing the captain and Sinter forward onto the deck and then down on the floor.

"We've hit something!" screamed Sinter.

The noise continued to wail, rage and tear in their ears, and the boat lurched erratically from side to side.

The captain fought back to his feet and ripped the

power levers back to idle the engines. Immediately the noise stopped, and the ship glided on in silence, the only sounds the muffled shouts of the crew as they scrabbled from their beds and rushed to their emergency procedures.

"No," the captain said grimly. "No, we haven't hit anything. Sadly, we've *been* hit. That was the props."

"The props?" Sinter asked.

"The main propellers. They've been snagged. Caught up in something. If they can't spin, the boat can't move."

They looked at each other, both knowing what had happened. The *Maru* had anticipated they would follow by night, and had used the cover of darkness to lay a fouling trap, a line of ropes, nets and buoys that would ensnare their propellers, and leave the *Saviour* adrift.

By now Mistral and a few other members of the crew had made it up to the bridge.

"So what's the damage, Captain?" she asked.

"We won't know till we get under the boat and look," the captain answered, "and we can't do that till daylight."

"So what do we do till then?" asked the posh girl, Katabatic. "Drop anchor and wait till sunrise?"

"We can't drop anchor," the captain replied bleakly, pointing at his charts. "The channels in between these islands are the deepest of their kind on earth. We're in two miles of water right now. And we sure don't have two miles of anchor line."

The crew all looked at each other, aghast.

"What, so we just drift around without control or power

until we hit something?" Katabatic's voice sounded panicked. "You've been telling us for weeks that these seas are the most treacherous on earth. Whirlpools, for God's sake! We have to abandon ship, take the *Galeocerdo* and get everyone out of here!"

The *Maru*'s plan had been brilliantly plotted, and perfectly executed. In deep water, unable to anchor or manoeuvre, the *Saviour* was in trouble. The straits in between the islands of Eastern Indonesia are not only deep but legendary for their currents, rip tides and raging white waters. And Katabatic wasn't wrong – in certain places, at the right times of day, huge whirlpools form that can suck smaller boats down to the bottom of the sea.

"We can't abandon," Mistral reasoned. "That's exactly what the *Maru* wants us to do. And if we all leave the *Saviour*, she'll be grounded, or sunk, and our mission will be over. Komodo's reefs will be smashed to pieces, these straits completely emptied of fish, dolphins, turtles . . ."

"We can't all leave," Sinter said.

There was a silence then, as they all looked to the captain. They knew him well enough to know that he was an honourable sailor and would, without doubt, live and die by the maxim that a captain should go down with his sinking ship. It was a sickening moment. The *Maru* had won. They had to flee for their lives, or face the consequences.

But then something simple came to Sinter. "Why do we have to wait for daytime to check the propellers?" she asked.

Katabatic scoffed, and rolled her eyes.

"The sea at night here is a lethal place," Mistral replied. "We don't have any dive lights, so you would be blind. With these currents, get swept away and you'd never be seen again. Not to mention that those sharks that were all friendly by day start to hunt by night. It's impossible."

"*Impossible* is to let the *Maru* get away with murder," Sinter retorted. "I want to try."

"That's just ridiculous," Katabatic complained in her pinched, plummy tones. "We only have one dive cylinder, and she barely knows how to use the thing at all!"

"Then you go," Sinter challenged, throwing down a gauntlet she knew would not be picked up. Katabatic dropped her eyes to the ground. She would not challenge again.

With that, the ship graunched and lurched to the side as it hit its first obstacle. Thankfully it wasn't huge, probably a floating buoy at the surface, but it was enough to send everyone staggering across the deck. A decision needed to be made, and fast.

The first problem to solve was light. "The squid boats don't have dive torches," reasoned Karma, a blonde-haired teenager from Texas with a cowgirl drawl. "They just hang big light bulbs over the water, and that's enough to bring up the squid. Maybe that'll work."

"But they won't be waterproof," said Damian the Irish lad, "so they can't go under. If they do, it'll dry our back-up generators and we'll lose power. And anyone in the water will get fried," he finished, somewhat grimly.

Damian and the three most technical crewmembers scuttled off to start tearing light bulbs out of their sockets and make long extension cables so they could be dangled over the side. The job was made harder by constant small collisions as the out of control *Saviour* clanged into ocean garbage. Without the engines, they were on back-up power and in near darkness.

As Katabatic talked Sinter through how the scuba setup worked, Sinter stripped to her bathing suit and pulled on dive fins.

"You'll need to be tethered, so you don't get carried away in the current," Mistral said, tying a line of rope around her waist and then up into a coil on the deck. "I'll be here, feeling as you go. Give me one tug for OK, two if you want more rope, three if you want us to pull you back in. I'll give you three tugs if I need you to come back."

Sinter's head was spinning as she tried to take in a week-long dive course in two minutes, on a ship swirling about out of control. Finally, the lights were rigged. They were hung on gaff poles down over the water, low enough to give some glow, yet not so much that they might accidentally dip in.

What am I doing? Sinter thought to herself for about the thousandth time. Taking her mask in her hand, she made to spit into it so it wouldn't fog up. Her mouth was totally dry. She looked around in despair.

"I ain't got no spit," she said to Mistral knowingly.

"Well, this is a test of true friendship," Mistral responded, spitting into the mask herself, and then rinsing it out with clear water. Out of nowhere, she grabbed the young girl and held her tightly. "Don't do anything dumb," she pleaded.

"My life is just one long run of dumb," Sinter replied, before pulling on her mask, placing the breathing regulator in her mouth, and stepping over the side.

10

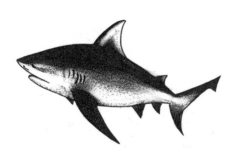

Ghostly green light wavered down through the inky black. Squadrons of squid with flashing light-shows ripping along their sides fired back and forth like cola-bottle torpedoes. Battling the urge to panic, Sinter sucked in through the breathing regulator and blew out clouds of bubbles, which erupted like mercury-encrusted balloons, expanding and pancaking their way towards the surface.

So many utterly new experiences at once, it was too much for her to take in. She could breathe – underwater! And she was diving at night. The lights from above illuminated an area no bigger than a squash court beneath the boat. Beyond its reaches the light became fog, then total darkness. Who knew what was lurking off beyond its fragile fingers? A tug on her safety line brought her back to reality. She felt for the loop at her belt, ran her fingers around till she found the rope, then tugged on it once in reply: "I'm OK."

She could already feel the force of the current on her face, ripping past at a brutal pace. She felt that if she turned her face slightly to the side, the flow would pull the mask off her face and the regulator from out of her mouth. Already, the rope was pulling tight, leaving her strung out like laundry on a line in a stiff breeze. She swung her head around to get her bearings. There, at the rear of the ship was the massive propeller, sheathed in a protective metal housing.

Driving against the current with her fins, Sinter swum up towards it, instantly aware that when she put in more effort, she sucked up more air from her scuba tank. She would need to be careful to watch her air gauge; it would be so easy to forget with so much on her mind. Running out of air under the ship at night was simply unthinkable.

Pulling herself up to the propeller, she groaned through her regulator. The *Maru*'s saboteurs had done their job well. The prop was tangled completely in chunks of old fishing gear. Some of it was rusting metal longlines she would have to untangle by hand, but there were also bits of rope and plastic netting.

Reaching down her ankle, Sinter drew out a wicked-looking dive knife, and started to saw her way through. After a few minutes, she remembered her air gauge and looked down.

A black and white phantom sliced through the gloom behind her. She gasped through her regulator. What was that? Heart beating faster and faster, she pulled herself up as close to the propeller as she could, trying to become invisible; but she knew any hunter of the midnight black would know she was there and would be her superior in every way. She was trapped here, with breathing apparatus she barely understood, battling the urge to scream.

The black shape flew past again. It was massive, as wide as a bus; long, pointed wingtips driving up and down with effortless ease, devil-like horns funnelling through the soupy sea.

It's a manta ray, Sinter suddenly knew, and horror became relief, and then utter awe. The lights below the boat had attracted a bloom of plankton in the water, and the manta had come in to feed on it, barrel-rolling over and over, driving water in through its gaping mouth, only for it to be strained out as it passed through the gills. These gill-rakers, sadly, have been the mantas' undoing, as they are highly prized in Chinese traditional medicine, believed to be a cure for asthma (for which they definitely do not work).

The manta flew, its wings undulating and swooping, propelling it through the darkness like an alien ship through the starry enchantment of space. The idea of anyone deliberately hunting a creature of such majesty, such ethereal glory, made Sinter stifle a sob.

Dragging herself away from the most incredible spectacle she had ever seen, Sinter returned to her work, cutting through the ropes and net. A big chunk came free, and Sinter near whooped with joy, before screaming with terror. Something yanked on her foot, something incredibly powerful, intent on dragging her down into the depths. In desperation she grabbed the prop shaft with one hand, but the grip on her foot tightened and hauled her downwards.

She swung her other hand up to grab the shaft, losing the knife in the process. It clanged off the hull, then drifted down into the deep. Following its trajectory down, Sinter's gaze landed straight on the eye of a monster – an eye as big as a tennis ball. Flashing white then deep red, tentacles lunging up towards her legs, was a gargantuan squid, easily as big as she was. The sucker cups that ran down its feeding arms had a tight grip on her ankle, the sharp teeth that line each sucker cup were shredding her flesh.

Blood was billowing out into the water – her own blood. As the squid tugged her, a cloud of brown ink emerged about it like smoke, hiding its terrible image. Its strength was formidable. And then, through the smoke, a lashing parrot-like beak emerged – its snapping, rasping, lacerating edges aimed at Sinter's legs.

She kicked down with her other foot, smashing the eye of the squid, but it didn't seem to feel any pain. It was too strong; she couldn't hold on. The squid was going to drag her down into the deepest waters. First her eardrums would burst, then her air would run dry, then the sinister creatures of the deep would tear her into tiny pieces. Sinter swung round to grab her line, to tug on it and call for help, but she never got the chance.

Suddenly there was another impact, a huge sidelong

crunch, and for a second the squid's grasp seemed to lose its power. Sinter chanced a look down. The squid's feeding arm was still attached to her ankle and beyond that the cloud of ink masked the rest of its body. But then, as the ink started to clear, the squid's arm floated free, severed – the squid was gone.

And then it smashed into the boat alongside her face, its empty eyes staring into hers. Sinter screamed and dropped the regulator from her mouth. The squid was smashed against the boat side again and again. Flashing teeth, grey and white, a huge thrashing tail . . . shark! The squid had been hit side on by a big bull shark, which was proceeding to tear it into tiny chunks. The squid was fighting back, but its beak was too far from the shark's body.

She had her chance. Sinter grabbed her regulator and thrust it back into her mouth. A quick glance at her air supply showed she had no more than two minutes left underwater before the tank ran dry. She had to work fast. Without the knife, she unravelled the wires and ropes by hand, focusing on her mission, refusing to look behind her at the titanic struggle taking place in the thrashing darkness.

Ropes and strings pinged free and unravelled, but the last wire just would not come loose; it was twisted right into the blades of the propeller. She fought with all her might, using her fear to find strength she didn't know she possessed. Finally it came off, and she swung around to see the bull shark tearing the chunks of its squid prey into pieces, ripping its bulldog-like snout side to side, turning the water milky with blue squid blood.

Sinter tried to calm herself. *Think!* She couldn't summon help – if the crew pulled her up on the line, the movement would attract the shark's attention, and then she'd be hanging at the surface, exposed, open to attack. She couldn't hang here – her air would run out and she would have to make for the surface.

The shark devoured the chunks of squid, then started to circle, snout snapping. It could still sense the blood in the water, was still hyper-stimulated, wanting to feed again. Sinter shifted, trying to draw herself even closer to the propeller, but the movement was enough to attract the shark's attention.

The lateral-line organ that runs down the length of a shark's body is lined with tiny, sensitive hairs, enough to detect the wake that's left behind by a fish as it swims away – and it sensed something nearby. Sinter battled to maintain her nerve. She mustn't give off signs of stress. She couldn't have an elevated heart rate or breathing – the shark would pick up on that, and it would know she was scared. Prey gets scared.

Instead, she breathed in and out deeply and calmly, much as she had done with her freediving training. She focused on lowering her heart rate, relaxed, and let go of the safety of the propeller. Then she simply drifted out into the shark's world, holding herself in as confident and commanding a position in the water as she could. She maintained the shark's gaze, keeping eye contact.

"I see you," she said. "You can't take me by surprise."

The shark kept on coming, nosing towards her, but cautiously now. Too close. Sinter struck out with a clenched fist, making impact on the sensitive snout of the bull shark. It wasn't expecting that! Clearly the pain wasn't too extreme, but the surprise was enough to make it turn, a swift tail sweep carrying it away from Sinter and off into the fog at the outer limits of the lights. Then it just kept on swimming, fading into the oily black, leaving her alone.

Sinter instantly gripped the line and heaved, three frantic tugs on the rope.

Back on the surface, Mistral was nearly pulled overboard with the force of the tugs. She could sense the panic transmitted through the line as if they were impulses pulsed down a nerve.

"Pull!" she screamed, and the entire crew became a tug of war team, hauling hand over hand, dragging Sinter upwards.

"Not too quickly," Katabatic countered. "She'll get bent."

Simple physics means that when you breathe in air underwater it is pressurised by the weight of water pressing in on it. If you surface too quickly, that air expands and can simply burst your lungs. If you've been down deep, then the tiny bubbles of air in your blood and joints expand

and can kill you, or leave you with permanent injuries, known in diving terms as "the bends".

Breathing was getting harder and harder. Sinter finally sucked on the mouthpiece and nothing came in return. She was out of air! Luckily, Sinter had not been deep. The lights above gleamed like giant super moons, tantalising her skywards.

She was back on the surface in seconds. As she broke through she ripped out the regulator and gasped, "Shark!"

That was enough to have calloused hands hauling her out, manhandling her over the guardrail with little dignity, but she couldn't have cared less. As soon as she lay panting on the deck, she held up a single thumb.

There was no cheer, just people scattering across the ship, all with their own jobs to do. Just minutes later, there was a charging sound, then chugging, then the lights guttered back into full power and finally the characteristic sounds of the propeller whirring into action. From every corner of the *Shark Saviour* came whoops of elation, people hugging and crying out with joy. The *Maru* hadn't won; they were alive.

Sinter shrugged her way out of the diving cylinder and fins and shivered to herself, for the first time aware of the breeze on her wet skin. She smiled. The bad guys would not win. Not while there were people around who believed.

People who were willing to give everything to save their planet.

11

Saker had his destination firmly in mind, but first he had to cross the entire length of Ukraine to get to the border with Poland. Although he looked pretty much like a local, he didn't speak a word of the language, and would stand out instantly as soon as someone tried to talk to him.

He took a turn to the north, travelling mostly by local buses, battered metal boxes full of people smoking acrid cigarettes, bumping over roads so potholed it seemed they were driving over the surface of the moon. Eventually, though, as they neared the border with Belarus the towns and villages thinned out and then, abruptly, there was nothing but forest.

The bus came to a standstill at one last stop, and the smiley, well-rounded and ruddy-cheeked driver bent forward to roll a lever that would change the destination board at the front of the bus, shifting her headscarf back from her forehead as she did so. Saker got up from his seat – by now he was the only person left on board – opened the door and stepped down onto the road.

A few hours later, having wandered down a lane without any sign of human beings, Saker came to two huge yellow and black signs on either side of the road. Off into the distance on either side ran reels of razor wire, a huge barrier enclosing whatever lay ahead.

He couldn't understand what was written on the signs, but he recognised the yellow circular symbol with what looked like a black propeller in the centre. It was the universal symbol for nuclear power, and for radioactivity. Elsewhere on the signs, someone had scrawled in black spray paint another circular symbol, with a black line down the centre, and an inverted V at the base: the symbol that has now come to mean "Peace", but was once the sign for nuclear disarmament.

The signs meant little to Saker, but he knew this place by reputation. This was the Chernobyl Exclusion Zone.

In 1986, long before Saker was born, Chernobyl was the site of the greatest ever human disaster. The nuclear power station there suffered meltdown and the reactor exploded, sending a vast cloud of radioactive fallout pouring over the surrounding country, and eventually over the entire continent.

Saker was about to enter the abandoned city of Pripyat, once home to fifty thousand souls. This had been the closest town to the nuclear reactor, and had been completely abandoned. The countryside for thirty miles in every direction remained empty of people, the perfect place for a fugitive to lose themselves. Despite the deeply frightening reputation of Chernobyl, he saw no skulls or skeletons, no dogs picking at long-dead, leathered flesh.

The town had been completely evacuated in the thirty-six hours after the explosion, and the only instant fatalities had been workers at the plant caught in the blast itself. The real cost had come later, much later, when the radioactivity had tainted the people caught in the fallout cloud.

Who knows how many hundreds of thousands had died horrible deaths as a result? Radioactive material takes millennia to break down, and the surrounding area would remain lethally tainted – possibly for the rest of human existence – testament to the horrors that our race have unleashed on nature. However, as long as you don't dwell too long, and don't happen to walk over some depleted uranium, then it is possible to pass through the Exclusion Zone without negative effects. And over the last thirty years, nature had begun to take back what was rightly hers.

Saker wandered the streets of the ghost town, his unlaced training shoes treading down the centre of a cracked main road that would once have thundered with cars and people. Normally his instinct would be to blend in to the background, walking along the side of the street, amongst the shop fronts and street vendors. But there was no one here to see him.

Plants had pushed their way up from beneath and erupted through the tarmac. Primroses bloomed yellow and cheerful against the grey, grey, grey of the remnant city. To one side a huge concrete office block loomed. It would have been without character or charm even in its bustling heyday, but now it was the very picture of gloom. Windows smashed, black smears of rainwater staining the frontage. A tattered, once red, now washed-out pink flag hung limp and lifeless outside the entranceway.

Saker tried to imagine it as it would have been the day before the tragedy; hundreds of office workers in their identical suits and work dresses, scuttling in and out of the revolving doors, chitter chattering to each other about nothing in particular, with no idea that their world was about to come to an end.

Suddenly, ahead of him, a shaggy grey-white dog strode out into the middle of the street. Something about it tugged at his brain, and then he realised: it wasn't just a dog – it was a wolf! A magnificent, male wolf, standing in broad daylight, its silver mane backlit in the middle of a city street. Saker knew through his experiences in Siberia that wolves around the world have been so persecuted by humankind that they have learned to be terrified of man and to stay as far away from him as possible.

They are active mostly by night, and would never approach human habitation. But here, in the middle of a once thriving city, the wolf had no man to fear. It lifted its muzzle and sniffed the air, eyes closing as if savouring the delight of a new scent. Then he turned and looked directly at Saker, his golden eyes full of mischief. He licked his lips, and sneezed.

"Bless you," Saker said.

The wolf looked at him again, looked away, then turned and trotted off down the centre of the road, huge paws padding on the cracked and faded yellow lines.

The already weak sunlight was beginning to fade, shadows growing tall, casting the shapes of phantom strangers on the cracked walls and pavements. Saker needed somewhere to spend the night and had to admit nowhere was looking particularly welcoming. Behind a wrought-iron fence was what had once been a school. In the yard outside, a climbing frame and swings. A deflated football sat disconsolate. It had probably been deserted mid-game, a young striker poised to score, then lifted up by the armpits and hauled away as the panic took hold. The open wooden doors to the school were painted dark blue, but the sorry paint had all but peeled away.

As he made to walk in, a huge hulking shape strolled out of the doorway, having to stoop its head to get beneath the frame. It was the size of a shire horse, glossy brown and with an impressive chandelier of antlers as broad as a sofa. A moose. The large animal chewed distractedly and eyed Saker with disinterest, its flubbery, floppy upper lip drooping over its munching molars.

In Europe moose are called elk, and the massive male

is the largest of all deer species. Saker was frozen still; in the autumn these big bulls can be extremely dangerous, as they are filled with testosterone, driven to fight with anything in their path. Now though, the moose clearly just wanted to find some nice green shoots to munch.

"Excuse me," a bemused Saker said, as he edged the massive flanks of the moose aside to enter in through the doorway. The moose shuffled slightly, looking back over its shoulder at Saker distractedly, as if to say, "I shouldn't bother, I've checked it out already – there's not enough grass to feed a fawn in there."

The walls were lined with scribbles and paintings, the prized work of toddlers long since departed. In one of the classrooms, rows of old-fashioned desks were lined up towards a blackboard, still scrawled with the chalk of that last school morning. It looked as if a bell could ring any moment, and a horde of phantom spectre children could flood in, chanting with echoing ghost laughter. Pens still rolled on desktops, the front desk still held the mug of the teacher's last cuppa, never drunk, and now sprouting what looked like watercress.

A once colourful Christian mural was painted on the far wall, a picture of a remarkably Ukrainian looking Jesus in white robes, standing with his arms spread in blessing, perfect halo around his head, fluffy clouds in the baby-blue sky. *Remarkable*, Saker thought, *that people always represent their gods in their own image.*

A sapling had sprung up through the floorboards and

was sprouting spring leaves out through the windows, growing from inside the building to outside. The wooden windowsill had rotted away, and shoots and flowers had sprung through the mulch, making bizarre natural window boxes. Looking out through the window, there was a shifting Ferris wheel, its chairs creaking, swinging back and forth for all eternity.

Beyond them, he could see the reactor itself: blue, white, rusting orange, its cooling towers no longer smoking, its domes and external stairways vacant, a mausoleum to the folly and destructiveness of man. To the east lay the so-called "Red Forest", the pine trees that were scorched red by the dust cloud that spewed from the reactor, still today remaining the most radioactive place on earth.

Staring at the bizarre vista, Saker's mind wandered to his own future. This abandoned town could be his last place of solace before throwing himself into the lion's den. Ironic that this, probably the most dangerous and frightening place on earth, was to him the safest. For the first time in years, he didn't need to be paranoid about who might be watching. He could relax, and let his mind wander.

With the shackles lifted, he was taken aback by the first image to pop into his head. It was Sinter. And not just any image of Sinter, but the Sinter that would star in a shampoo commercial, amber eyes glinting like precious gems, glossy sleek hair blowing in the wind . . . Saker snorted. That was ridiculous! Sinter never looked like that! Most of their time together they'd been smeared in mud and sweat and on the run.

But why would her image come to him so readily? Perhaps it was because he was so utterly alone. Having no one to talk to had never bothered him before. The Clan boys had always taken their comfort in solitude. After all, many of their totem animals were solitary their whole lives. Do they feel lonely? Does a polar bear spending its whole life wandering across the Arctic tundra feel sad and alone? They certainly don't seek out other polar bears for company. If they do meet other bears outside of breeding seasons, they battle, sometimes to the death.

If wild predators didn't feel lonely, then why should he? But that didn't stop the fact that right now he just wanted someone to talk to. He wanted to chat about this remarkable place, about his fear for what might lie ahead. For the first time, he wanted to share the excitement and the terror, to put it in words for someone else to listen to and understand.

And not just anyone, he realised. He wanted Sinter. Her capacity to listen, to never just try and solve other people's problems before she had begun to understand them. Looking around at the broken down buildings that would have to provide his sleeping-place for the night, he longed for the warmth of Sinter, lying beside him.

Wandering through the abandoned school, he entered a space where the ceiling had fallen through from a room above that had clearly been a library. The floor was littered with tumbled books, their paper pages yellowing and curling, gaudy coloured covers torn and tatty. A child's doll stared blankly at Saker from its blue plastic eyes.

His heart jumped, instantly on his guard, remembering that in a warzone seemingly innocent items like this are often booby-trapped with explosives. But though it felt like it, this wasn't a warzone. There would be no grenade lurking beneath. He took the doll in his hands. The plastic was starting to bleach, its synthetic shock of blonde hair framed a frozen, toothless grin. As he lifted it, its eyelids closed, blinking lifelessly. A shudder ran up his spine. What had happened to the child who last played with this doll? Were they still alive? Disfigured by radiation? Or were they a healthy adult with a family of their own, knowing only of what happened here from the stories and old photographs?

In the gymnasium, he found some old training mats to make a bed. His duvet was formed from old children's duffel coats still hanging on their named and numbered hooks. Anyone else would have barely slept a wink in this nightmare town, but for Saker it was the only place on earth he knew he would not be pursued. He fell asleep within minutes, and slept like a dead man.

He was woken at dawn by an unearthly squealing, a noise like a tortured nightmare. A six-strong sounder of brown, furry, wild boar with crested manes snuffled in the remnants of allotments outside the tenement buildings. Stepping outside, a dark shadow fell briefly over him and he looked up. High above, the broad wings of a white-tailed eagle blocked out the thin sun. It appeared to have a deer fawn hanging in its talons.

As Saker watched, it threw its wings forward and landed in a huge messy nest of untidy branches in the top of a red-painted bell tower. Saker watched as the bird tore chunks of meat off the deer fawn and fed it to the two ugly, begging chicks sat inside the nest.

He looked to where the sun was rising in the east. His course was the opposite direction, due west, away from the light. As he reached the outskirts of what was once the city centre, the tumbledown streets gave way to open fields of thigh-high grass, with the remains of what had once been the homes of farmers and labourers. Some of the buildings were sinking into once-drained swamps; barn doors swung open on creaking hinges and dovecotes leaned at improbable angles, now home to nesting dormice.

As Saker wandered through the fields, he came across herds of wisent or European bison, gigantic hairy beasts that could barely lift their own massive heads and horns. The few places they still exist, they stampede at the sight of a human. Here, in this forgotten, deserted place, they didn't even lift their snouts as he passed. Even more wondrous, a herd of shaggy brown wild horses trotted past before him, Przewalski's horses, some of the only truly wild horses left on the planet.

"How much better the world is without us," Saker found himself saying out loud. "Chernobyl was perhaps our greatest mistake, our most destructive moment, but nature bounced back."

And it was true. Against all the odds, even here in this scorched, violated place, without man and his ceaseless desire to take, take, take . . . nature found a way to return.

12

The powerboat hurtled over the waves, warm spray peppering their faces, sun glinting fiercely off the sea surface. Big black skua birds hung in the dead air alongside their hull, barely needing to flap their wings to keep pace. These midair pirates will catch other birds on the wing, shaking them by the leg until they vomit up their fish catch, which the skua will then swoop and devour. It was revolting, and somewhat cruel, but you had to admire their flying skills.

With her propeller freed, the *Shark Saviour* had made up great time on the *Maru*, and caught up with the ship as it entered the national park. The *Maru* had slowed to drop its nets and longlines, giving its chasers the advantage. The speedboat launched from *Shark Saviour* in a hurry before tearing out through the small islands, past small, brightly painted wooden boats which trundled out to sea every night to catch squid by torchlight.

The team had always struggled to directly engage the enemy, usually just focusing on the carnage left behind as the factory ships carved through the ocean, taking everything alive. However, this time they had hit the jackpot. As soon as they were out beyond the islands they saw through binoculars a huge ship the length of a football field, with rusting orange flanks and a funnel amidships chugging black smoke. Because of its size, it barely seemed to be moving, but the powerboat had to be at top speed to keep pace with it.

The *Maru*'s crew were old hands at dealing with saboteurs, and were up on deck, waiting. Cloaked in bright orange oilskins, they stood around water cannons like movable machine-gun mounts. They also carried fouling mechanisms; those same lengths of old fishing gear that had worked their effect on the *Shark Saviour*. These would be hurled into the water, with the aim of tangling the propellers of the chasing boats. They'd also be carrying bucket-loads of foul-smelling rotting shark guts to hurl overboard onto the smaller boat.

But it would take more than a bad smell to deter the chasers. The *Galeocerdo* held a mixture of similar weapons to try and stall the efforts of the larger longlining boat. The *Shark Saviour*'s golden rule, though, was that no one was to be hurt. Precious as the marine world was, they could never risk a human life in the conflict. *Shark Saviour* was funded by donations, all from benefactors who believed their cause was good.

Those donations would soon dry up if anyone actually got hurt.

Sinter felt her blood pulsing with the thrill of the chase. Finally she was going to get a chance to do battle with the people she was learning to hate. But before they could gain ground on the ship, they sped up on the longline, and inevitably there was work to be done.

"Big shark!" yelled Mistral. "It's being dragged but still moving, not dead yet."

The captain risked leaning away from the wheel to get a look at the shape below them. "It's a tiger!"

Sinter's ears pricked up. Her very own totem animal! After her adventures in the forests of Borneo, the local people had named her Tigress and given her a tribal tattoo to celebrate her christening. Tigers had been precious to her ever since, but she didn't know there was a sea tiger. This she had to see. Rushing to the railing, she looked down at a grey shape alongside them.

"Easy there, girl." Mistral was at her shoulder. "This isn't one of those sweet reef sharks. Tiger sharks can bite clean through a turtle shell. This isn't one to mess with."

"But it's dying," Sinter protested. "I'm going to cut it loose."

"It's been dragged for miles," the captain said. "The thing will be out of fight. It's fine, Mistral – let her help."

Seeing that she was determined, the Maori girl nodded her agreement.

"With sharks we leave the hooks in," the captain

explained. "They're tough enough that they can survive with it in their mouths, and it's not worth losing an arm over."

Not having to cut through the hook meant they could simply use bolt cutters to go through the line, and release it. Sinter leaned over the guardrail to hold the by now familiar sandpaper skin as the others worked on slicing through the line. With a loud *ping* the line came free, and the shark was liberated, but lying leaden and lifeless alongside them.

Clasping it by the dorsal fin, Sinter could see the dark stripes that ran vertically down its body, giving it its name. It gaped open its vast maw as if gasping for air, showing off the curved, can-opener teeth that it uses for carving through shell and bone. It was simply one of the most dramatic things she had ever seen, but there was no doubt the shark had nearly given up its fight. Its few movements were fading, the odd half-hearted kick from the tail, but it was clearly beyond exhausted.

"Someone's going to have to swim it," said Manta, one of the youngest of the crew, as if this was the most natural thing on earth.

"Swim a five-metre tiger?" asked Mistral. "You can count me out."

"What does that mean?" Sinter asked.

"Most sharks need to swim to be able to breathe," explained the captain. "It washes water into their mouths, then over their gills. When they can't swim, they can't breathe and they asphyxiate. A bit like when you can't breathe underwater."

Sinter nodded to show she understood.

"So when we catch one, and it's almost dead," Mistral continued, "the last chance is to grab a hold of it and swim it through the water, helping it breathe. It works on the small ones, but no one's ever tried with one this size. If it woke up and tried to bite you, you wouldn't stand a chance."

"I want to do it," Sinter stated with absolute certainty. "And before you say anything," she continued, looking at Mistral now, "yes, I know what I'm doing; and no, I'm not going to be sensible and stay on board."

Mistral nodded. She was starting to learn that there was an awful lot more to the young Indian girl than first met the eye. Sinter stripped down to her bathing suit, tossing her clothes aside.

"Now does someone mind explaining what the hell I'm about to do?" Sinter asked.

Having been advised to approach from the tail end, staying behind the mouth, Sinter slipped over the side, keeping hidden the fear she didn't want to admit to the rest of the crew. The waves splashed her up against the skin of the shark, grazing her skin off. That, combined with the previous attentions of the squid tentacles, meant her lower legs were starting to look a right mess.

I wonder if the blood in the water will bring any more sharks in? she thought, before giggling to herself. If only Saker could see her now – he wouldn't believe the transformation in her.

Now she was in the water alongside the shark, she could see how big it really was. It was as long as a car, thick as a pony, dark above and light beneath in the classic marine colouration called countershading. When you looked down at the shark from above, it would blend into the deep blue sea beneath it. When it swam overhead, the shark would shine white with the bright sky above.

The monster shark twitched. Saker could feel the huge muscles contract beneath her palms, but they were sluggish.

What am I doing? Sinter asked herself for the thousand and first time. She'd been told to take a grip of the shark around the dorsal fin and just start swimming, driving it down into the deep.

At the surface, she breathed as calmly as possible. "Out with the bad air, in with the good," she chanted to herself, filling her blood up with life-giving oxygen. "So weird that we both need the same thing, but I get it from air, and you get it from water," she told the shark, for once not caring whether her colleagues on board thought she was weird, "but you can't live in my world, and I can't live in yours."

Finally, she took a last deep breath, ducked her face into the cool water, and started to swim. Once released from the helping hands above, the shark started to sink. Its supremely hydrodynamic shape eased it through the water with slick ease. But it needed to be propelling itself.

Sinter swam for all she was worth, dragging the huge

beast, willing it to kick back into life with every cell in her body. But it was no good – she needed to breathe, and to continue down any further would drown the both of them. Just as it seemed she could not swim another stroke, there was movement, a single sweep of the long tail . . . and the shark was in motion.

Sinter's heart leapt, first with joy, as the immense predator came back to life beneath her fingertips, then with fear that it might simply turn and tear her to shreds. But instead, the majestic beast swept its body side to side and vanished into the Blue.

At the surface, gasping for air, Sinter was hauled aboard unceremoniously by many hands, crewmates questioning if she was all right, laughing, slapping her back, congratulating her for her guts. Mistral stood back till the others were done, then took her in a huge bear hug. "That was nuts – don't ever do that to me again."

"I don't like to break up the party," the captain's voice was full of authority, yet there was a hint of a waver to it, "but we've got company."

The crew all turned round, not really comprehending what he was saying. It didn't make any sense – they'd taken at least twenty minutes to free the big tiger; the factory longlining ship should be miles away by now. Sinter moved next to the captain so she could see where he was pointing and gasped. Bearing down on them, no more than a few hundred metres away and covering the space in between them by the second, was what appeared to be a huge, floating, rusty city. The big ship had turned right around and was heading straight at them, with a direct course that seemed to suggest this was no accident.

"Good God, they're going to ram us," whispered the captain.

13

The engines sputtered into effect, before roaring as the captain rammed the throttles down and accelerated them towards their foe. For a second this seemed to be madness, but there was no choice, the speedboat could only manoeuvre while going forward at speed, which meant he had no option but to hurtle headfirst towards their foe, playing a high-speed game of chicken with a boat that could crumple them like matchsticks.

The crew on board yelled with horror as the huge ship loomed over them, thousands of tonnes of iron behind a pointed prow aimed like a weapon. The name of the ship glowered down like a threat in human-sized, white letters: *Moumoku Maru*.

"Hang on!" shouted the captain, throwing the wheel sideways as the shadow of the ship blocked out the sun. The speedboat leapt sideways, banking away from the towering hull, which thundered past like an oversized freight train. Suddenly everything was silent, as the constant roar of the wind was shut out by the colossal windbreak. But then the air was torn apart by the foghorn of the factory ship. The crew clasped their hands over their ears, desperate to block out the dread blast of the horn.

Then abruptly the wind roared again. They were clear. The huge ship had passed. They were back in open sea and banking hard away from its mighty mass.

Too late, the captain saw his mistake. Behind the ship was a wall of water, the wake displaced by a ship that weighed more than a skyscraper. They hit the wave at top speed and banked over to the right, so it spun them in the air, flipping the speedboat completely. For the second time in a matter of minutes, Sinter hit the sea, but this time gulped in a breath of seawater.

She surfaced, gasping through the salt burn to the back of her throat, choking to breathe. The second wave of the wake crashed over her like a Tsunami, sweeping the overturned speedboat backwards, the hull suddenly on top of her. The next wave lifted her as if she was weightless, and planted her on top of the upturned boat. She clung to it desperately, fingernails clawing down its plastic flanks, greasy with green algae.

Another wave exploded over her, and another, and then the sea started to calm. It felt as though saltwater had flooded through her veins and poured out of her nose, its bitter scour stinging her eyes and lungs. The shock was wearing off, and she could feel there were no major injuries, but now that she was safe and alive, there was a plunging feeling in her stomach. Where were her colleagues? The captain? Manta and Mistral? Had they all been drowned? Where were they?

Before she had a chance to scan the sea around, once again the wind and spray were shattered by a sound so low it seemed to vibrate her very bones. The ship had turned and was bearing down on her once more, its foghorn blasting.

Sinter wiped the water and sodden hair from her face. This couldn't be happening. The ship was coming back to finish the job. It was going to ram the boat again and send her straight to the bottom of the sea, where she would be food for the crabs. There was no point trying to swim for it, she would never be able to get clear of the down drag caused by a ship that size.

There was no hope, except for human connection. Sliding about on the slimy boat hull, Sinter found her way to her knees then, faltering, to standing. She held her arms aloft, waving at the colossal ship, just praying someone on board would see her and relent. The foghorn sounded again, a deep, deafening bass that inspired dread. And still it kept coming, the axe-edge of the prow aimed at her.

That's probably the greatest overkill in history, she thought. *Using a sledgehammer to squash an ant.*

Big ships don't manoeuvre easily, but the factory ship started to turn – with the sound of straining metal, flexing wires and the mighty propeller and, once more, the foghorn of doom.

Sinter closed her eyes, and waited for death to take her. But the impact never came. The ship slowed, the wave at its prow subsiding, engine noises abating, the speed now only coming from momentum. Now the boat was alongside her, and she looked up the hull, like the walls of a monumental building. Way above, the stick-figure silhouettes of men were standing looking down.

Perhaps she had not been killed yet, but Sinter doubted there would be much of a welcome party.

14

Yet another new country, and it was like being transported back in time to the Middle Ages. Farmers still made their way down the rutted dirt roads in horse-drawn, rattling carts; old men sat smoking outside cottages cut from crude blocks of stone, watching the world go by. The Carpathian Mountains, capped in snow, loomed over the landscape like a hulking threat or glowering, white-haired trolls. And for the first time, Saker saw the ancient forest.

These vast woodlands would once have stretched across the entirety of Europe, but have been cut back as man, ever-hungry, advanced across the continent. Even today, though, expanses exist with dark corners where man feels like a stranger, and wolves, lynx, wild boar and bear roam.

At the outskirts, the lower branches of trees were strimmed chest-high by the browsing of dappled deer; butterflies danced erratically about the delicate slipper-shaped blooms of orchids, and lusty-voiced birds were in full song. Once he'd ducked inside, the forest was like a dense green grotto, with moss-covered trunks and roots like witch's fingers, the canopy above cutting out any light. Soon the birdsong was deadened by the vegetation, and Saker's footfalls were silent in the spongy sphagnum moss.

It was the primeval forest of a Grimm's fairy tale, the kind of place where a tree could suddenly come to life and crush you in its gnarled fingers, or where a tribe of evil sprites could pluck your hair and lead you to disorientated doom, lost for ever in the jade caverns.

Saker, however, knew he was home. Crushing the grass in between his fingertips, he drew in the scent. Instantly he was back in the world of his childhood. The sense of smell is the closest linked to memory in the human brain, and has the greatest power of any of the senses to take you to a time in your past. Saker saw himself running around the forest, other boys leaping and darting about him. Far from a childhood game, the faces were twisted into snarls, teeth bared like fangs, sinews taut.

This place had been home: the classroom and dojo where he'd trained to become Clan, where he'd acquired his falcon totem animal, and learned to perform with its skills. Somewhere here would be what he was looking for, the answer to all his questions.

As he wandered, he plucked familiar nuts from the ground and chewed on edible greens with a sharp citrus flavour. He noticed the tracks of deer, fox and badger in the mud and, without thinking, his mind was processing the story – what animal had left their mark here, how long ago, what condition they were in. Sinter had tried to coax his gentler side into existence, but the hunter in him was too deeply ingrained. It was in his nature to pursue, to run down and then to dominate.

After a few hours' walking, Saker reached into his pocket and took out Wolf's phone. He'd avoided turning it on till now, as he was sure it would be traced, and his movements followed. But now he engaged it, and switched on the GPS device. Not surprisingly, it failed to locate any satellites under the dense canopy of the trees, so Saker began casting around in search of an open meadow.

When he found one, it was to another bombardment of sensory overload and memory. The white and pink flowers within were only found in such secluded forest clearings. Dried rabbit droppings crumbled between his fingers. He didn't need to gorge himself to be sated on the acorns and berries, just the smell was enough. When the sky was visible, Saker orientated the phone upwards, and waited.

Finally there was a beep, as it connected to enough satellites to get a fix on his position. Looking at the GPS co-ordinates, he realised how close he was. He knew this had all seemed familiar! Perhaps this meadow was the very one Wolf had been taken to by the Prophet. Perhaps his comrades and colleagues who had failed the Clan were buried beneath his feet right here. Involuntarily, Saker felt a shiver running up his neck. Suddenly this place gave him the creeps. He decided not to stay long, and to keep moving.

An hour or so more, and things started to become even more familiar. Little rabbit trails led over fallen birch trees. Tiny streams trickled over smooth stones, like a cobbled street on a rainy day. Now Saker's whole approach changed – he was stalking a foe he couldn't see.

He shod his shoes and socks so he'd be lighter on his feet, treading each footfall with care to avoid creating a telltale twig snap. His senses were so focused it was almost as if he was straining to hear a rabbit twitching its nose or a deer's heartbeat. He had to move as if a Clan member was watching behind every tree, moving to the forest's rhythm.

Ahead of him, between the green trunks, he saw something that was burned into his memory: sandstone rock outcrops in amongst the vegetation, the rock green with moss and algae, rivulets of water dripping down its sides. This place seemed so familiar! It had definitely been a part of his childhood. Treading more lightly still, spreading his weight across his whole foot so as not to create too much impact, he crept closer, eyes flicking around him for anything untoward.

As he approached the rock, he could see the sides were uneven, rippling with crannies and crevices. A slot became visible, tight for a fully-grown man, but easily achievable for Saker when he turned his shoulders sideways. Heart careering around inside his chest, he stepped into the vertical crack, and moved inside. The slot ran for about ten metres, twisting from side to side, before abruptly coming to an end.

The wall in front of him was orangey-yellow rock with a faded green hue to it, lumpy, misshapen. Saker reached out with his hands and traced the rock with his fingers. The roughness beneath his fingertips felt normal, but there was something wrong. The rock wasn't cool to the touch. Saker braced himself, and pushed. The rock simply slid backwards, and creaked open like a heavy barn door.

Behind the fake rock door, a dark passage led off into the rocky outcrop. Hewn from the natural sandstone, its walls were dank and cave-like, musty smelling. Saker took the small torch from his pocket, and switched it on. It cut a beam through the tunnel, dust particles in the air dancing and twirling in the light.

As he progressed, still placing each footfall with extreme care, he noticed CCTV cameras on the walls above him. They didn't move or come to life with little red recording lights; they just stared down at him almost mournfully, like sentinel robots left to perform a task, then forgotten for millennia.

Expecting any second the warning lights to come blaring on and armed Stormtroopers to explode from the shadows, Saker's head twitched from side to side with every drip from the rock roof. Abruptly, the tunnel came to an end, with a wire mesh door and a gaping shaft beyond.

It was an old-fashioned lift, like the ones that used to carry coal miners from the surface down into the bowels of the earth. Saker took a deep breath, grabbed a hold of the mesh, slid it to one side and stepped in. The floor of the lift was constructed of a metal grate, darkness beneath. Above him, steel cables led to the pulleys and winding mechanisms. The lift itself was little more than a metal bucket, swinging about in the black chasm.

Saker shone his torch around some more. To one side was a hanging operational panel with two buttons on it – one for up, one for down. Taking a deep breath, he took it in his hands and pressed the down button. Nothing happened. He pressed it again. Then again. He tried the other button, then frantically pressed them both over and over again. No results.

He blew out a long sigh – partly released tension, with a bit of relief thrown in for good measure. It seemed inevitable that what he sought was below him, but there was no way of getting there. After standing and thinking for what felt like an eternity, he finally looked up at the wires above, and then down beneath the cage. There was another wire, leading down. He closed his eyes and muttered to himself through gritted teeth, "Not again."

Taking his torch in his teeth, Saker swung one leg over the side of the cage, then the other, and found himself on the outside. Looking down, he traced his possible hand-and foot-holds with his eyes, running through the moves he would need to make in his head, like a mountaineer assessing his route.

Taking hold of the base of the cage in both hands, he lowered his body down over the side until his feet swung free, then his legs and, at last, his whole weight dangled beneath the lightly swinging cage. Next he began swinging himself, trying to generate some momentum, becoming a giant pendulum, getting a little further each time towards the steel line.

Finally he snagged the line with one foot, pulled himself towards it and hooked the other leg around as well. He let go of the cage with one hand and, hanging by the other, he reached out towards the cable. Not quite! He missed, and swung free again, quickly grabbing the cage with both hands before he lost his grip and plunged.

He half squealed in fear, and the torch slipped from his teeth and tumbled. It bounced once, twice, the beam spiralling through the dusty darkness like a laser beam. There was a distant clang as it bounced once more, then an even more distant clang, then total and utter black.

15

Lightning really does strike twice. It was more than a year now since Saker had descended solo into the darkness of the sinkhole in Borneo and had nearly lost his sanity to the claustrophobia. He had felt the fear ever since. Even thinking about darkness and enclosed places made a sense of dread close in on his consciousness, and the sweat bead on his upper lip.

The only way he could find a way down into that cave in Borneo was by clambering down a cascade of natural vines. This time he had to do the same using a steel cable not much wider than his thumb, which now he couldn't even see.

Once more focusing himself on the task, Saker swung out with his feet again, and this time he caught the cable immediately. Reaching and feeling around for the line was somewhat easier now, as he wasn't visually aware of the drop below. Fumbling around, his thumb slapped the line, and he greedily grabbed out at it, wrapping his fingers around it. Then, ever so gingerly, he let go with his other hand and reached across to take a hold. With his whole body curled around the cable, he started to move downwards, into a Hades he couldn't see.

That kind of descent, hand over hand, is much harder than it looks. It would be easy to just let yourself slide, but there's so little traction on a metal wire, you'd soon gather speed then lose control and plummet to your death. So he went slowly, wiping his hands every few seconds to dry out the sweat and stop himself slipping. All the while, the demons seemed to close in around him, his dread of the dark, and of confined spaces, were now his constant companions. His battle was to ensure they didn't become his masters.

Down, down, down into uncertainty, not a glimmer of light, or the smallest sense of when it might end. But then his feet touched down. And not to rock, but to an earthen base. Keeping a hold on the cable in case this was some trickery of the dark, he fumbled about with his feet, finding the dimensions of solidity below him. It was ground. Letting go, he dropped to his knees, gasping with effort and building terror. What now?

On his hands and knees, he began to feel around on the elevator shaft floor. His heart was pumping so hard it seemed fit to drive itself out of his chest. His racing imagination saw scorpions and giant centipedes just beyond his touch, huge venomous snakes set to race over his hands and plunge their fangs into his exposed skin.

"Get a hold of yourself," he scolded, "this is Europe, not Borneo."

There would be nothing toxic out there in the black, nothing more dangerous than his own fear. Stopping, with his eyes clenched tight shut, he concentrated on his breathing, forcing himself to relax. "This is not a problem; you've got this," he told himself. At that second, his fingernail nudged something metal, which rolled away from him.

He reached out once more, finding a small narrow tube. His torch! Picking it up eagerly, he found the power button, and flicked it on. It was dead. Orientating the torch in his hands, he found the light end and, micro-millimetre by micro-millimetre, taking exquisite care not to lose any part, he unscrewed it, fiddled around with the batteries, then dropped them back in again. Tightening it up, he tried the power switch. Dead! In frustration he yelled at the Hades around him, and shook it angrily in his hands. It flickered into life.

Saker could have wept. Granted, the beam was weaker than before, and sputtered in and out of life, but it was light and, in total darkness, a little light goes a long way. He would have taken a single firefly in a jar!

"In the kingdom of the blind," said Saker to himself, "the one-eyed man is king."

He shone the light around his prison to find its dimensions. On three sides, the artificially mined walls rose vertically, but in front of him there was a chest-high ledge, leading to another passage. Gritting the torch between his teeth again, he clambered up over it, and into the tunnel beyond.

This next passageway was very different to the one at ground level up above his head. The walls were white plastic, with windowless doors every ten metres or so. Each one had no handle or keypad, but a blank pad alongside it that was probably a retinal or fingerprint scan. If it hadn't been for the lack of illumination, he could have been in the corridors of the Pentagon, or of a high-level research facility.

There was a squeal from a corner making him jump out of his skin. Flashing his torch around, it caught burning red eye-shine. A rat! He breathed out in relief. The rat turned and scampered off down the corridor, before making an abrupt turn at one of the doors and disappearing. Saker made his way down to the door, and slipped his fingers to the side of the frame. It was ajar just a fraction, and he carefully levered it open. Torchlight probing into the darkness, he stepped into what was clearly a computer lab.

Several banks of computer screens ran in rows the length of the small room. On the walls were world maps, both topographical and political. Pins and strings littered them, clearly planning for various missions. There were bookshelves stacked with scientific textbooks. The computers looked a little out of date. He ran a thumb over one of the screens and it carved a trail through the thick dust that had accrued there.

None of this was ringing any bells for Saker, not like the forest had done. All of childhood memories were of living amongst the trees, sleeping out in lean-tos, tree houses and hammocks through the summer, and ice caves and tents in the winter. Training martial arts amongst the saplings, tracking animals amongst the ferns and nettles.

He ran his fingers down the spines of some of the well-thumbed books on the shelves: *Venoms and Poisons of Marine Animals*; *Human Athletic Performance at Extreme High Altitude*; *Pack Hunting Strategies in Wolves and Orca*. He felt as if he could recite their contents word for word, as every title had been an integral focus of his training, but this place . . . it just didn't seem familiar at all.

Stepping back out into the corridor, he continued to wander on. By now he was confident the place was deserted, and was less careful about each footfall, but he was still beading with sweat from the fear his torch might die at any second.

A few doors down was another one which had been left slightly ajar. He stepped inside, and stopped dead in his tracks. The room within was a surgical operating theatre. A variety of machines lined the walls – dials and displays, wires and buttons. One wall was lined with a compact chemistry lab, with grubby test tubes and funnels, centrifuges, and racks of vials and flasks. A huge lamp hung from the ceiling above a padded operating table, which was dead centre of the space. A vision sparked in Saker's mind as if he'd been electrocuted. He knew this place.

As if sleepwalking, he stumbled over to the table. A flash frame in his brain: surgeons in white with their lower faces masked, glasses covering their eyes, all leaning in towards him, staring into his soul. A jolt, and the vision was gone. He ran his palm down the length of the table, gathering dust.

At the centre of the table was a broad leather belt, designed to strap the occupant down, and padded cuffs. This sparked another flash frame, this time seen from the outside looking in, an unknown form on this same operating table – crowded in by surgeons, screaming like a tethered beast, fighting to break free of the restraints.

Saker shook the horror free one more time, but there was no getting away from his certainty; he'd been here before. Closing his eyes, he willed the visions to return. Now he saw again the surgeons crowding in on their battling patient. One raised a syringe high in the air. It was as if he was a demonic high priest wielding a ceremonial dagger over some condemned animal. The operating table was his altar.

Saker flinched in horror, his eyes opened and the vision faded. He forced himself to concentrate. There was the operating theatre again – white, lit, working. The machines around the walls pinged and beeped, a drip bag gurgled and dribbled fluid down a line and into a vein. He focused on the vein, on the arm. Suddenly, it wasn't the arm of an adult patient any more, but the arm of a small boy, no more than a toddler. He was crying out in pain as the surgeons worked on him.

Saker focused on his face, on the twisted, contorted features. As he looked on, the image in his head flickered, as if it had been retuned. Suddenly he was looking into his own face.

Slamming the door behind him, Saker leaned back against the corridor wall, heart racing, breath pounding. His need to learn as much as he could from the underground research facility was tempered by the overwhelming horror he felt every second he stayed here. He decided to gather as much information as he could, then get back into the sunlight as soon as was possible.

At the end of the corridor was one more room with an open door. He swung the door open, and walked inside. What was inside was like a museum of zoological curiosities. On pedestals around the room were glass cylinders, stretching up to the ceiling. Inside, sunken in clear fluid, were milky-eyed dead animal specimens, a smorgasbord of the weird and wonderful from across the natural world.

Saker wandered between the tubes in bemused fascination. One held the twisted form of a shark pup, pressed lifeless against the glass. Saker's own reflection gleamed back at him, stretched and morphed as if in a House of Fun mirror. Beyond the reflection, the form of an ocelot, bunched into the bottom of its cylinder. Much of the lustre had bleached from its fur over time, but the rosette spots still stood out against the milky fawn of its base colour. A twisted snake that Saker knew to be a death adder curled up in the bottom of the next cylinder, and a long, ferret-like form with a dark mask across its eyes – a polecat – was encased in another.

All the animals had lost their majesty in death and had become grotesqueries, nightmare trophies, a peculiar freakshow. What did it mean? A few animals were too large to have complete specimens in jars, so here was a bear's head, separated from its body, staring lifelessly into space for all eternity. And next to it was a leg and paw, complete with claws, from what appeared to be a tiger. What was this place?

In the very last tube was a sight that caught the breath in the back of his throat. It was a bird, bedraggled sodden feathers plastered against the glass. As he circled around it the hairs started to tingle on the back of his neck. Curved talons and toes designed to grip told him it was a bird of prey. The sharp end to the wings said in life it would have been fast. The speckled colours, so faded here in the embalming fluid, would have been chestnut and amber in life. Following the curve of the animal around, he finally saw the head. A sharply curved beak, a dark streak across the eyes and a mahogany brown cap. His eyes met his own distorted reflection in the glass.

The very last conversation he'd had with Sinter, she'd said some very strange things. "You're so like your totem animals. Didn't you ever wonder about that?" she'd asked.

Saker had been baffled, unwilling to listen. "I am a falcon. I've spent so many years being trained like one that I've sort of become one."

Sinter had pressed him even further. "Maybe you feel half falcon, because you are. Because somewhere along the line someone actually mixed you with a bit of falcon."

Saker had refused to listen, had stormed out in utter fury, but here, face to face with the preserved specimen of his own totem animal, suddenly it seemed the only answer.

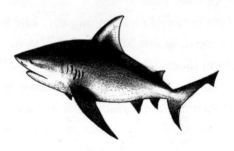

On board the *Moumoku Maru*, Sinter was facing an equally horrific realisation. All of a sudden, her survival was dependent on the very people she had been trying to sabotage. And not only her own survival, but that of her friends, who had disappeared without trace.

What she saw on board the ship sickened her to her stomach. The sweet, sickly stench of death clung to the nostrils. Blood was being hosed off the deck continuously. She had been brought aboard at the rear of the ship where the endless longlines were being hauled up over towering pulley systems. A hoard of men in orange oilskins stained black with old blood used gaff hooks to drag in the carcasses of every imaginable animal that could be found in the sea.

On the deck in front of her was the bulk of a minke whale, misshapen and grotesque in death. Two men stood on its back with long-handled flensing knives, removing the blubber from its body. Then there were the prize fish, such as massive tuna, the size of cows without their legs. These open-sea speedsters could fetch tens of thousands of dollars per fish on the Japanese fish market, and were being packed into vaults of ice just seconds after being pulled from the ocean. But it was the sharks that were the most shocking spectacle.

To one side, the sharks were being pulled up on their hooks, then their fins were hacked off with machetes before the bodies were simply slid across the deck and out through holes in the gunwales to drop into the crashing surf below. It was exactly as Mistral had said. These whole, huge, magnificent beasts killed for a tiny triangle of gristle, then discarded like a big grey banana skin.

The men even looked like pirates; skins tanned walnut brown from the constant tropical sun, colourful bandanas and caps over unkempt hair, dreadlocked or tangled. They sported tattoos and moustaches and jeered as she walked past, the weird hippy who had cut their lines and freed their catch.

"Finally," one spat in a thick accent, "we get to have a galley slave to clean up round here."

Another picked the guts out from a tuna he was slicing up, and threw them at her. The wet red slop hit her full in the chest, some spots spattering into her face. It was still warm, the animal thrashing around on the deck not even dead. Sinter was determined not to give them the satisfaction of seeing her flinch in disgust.

She wanted to vent her fury at the men who had deliberately sunk their boat, had tried to kill her and had possibly killed Mistral and the others. But she was under no illusions. There was nothing stopping these people from throwing her overboard. These factory ships were operating in a new Wild West: the open ocean. There was no police force and no one telling them what to do. There were supposed to be rules governing how they did things, but they paid them no heed. They were pirates, pirates stealing from the sea, plundering from every nation whose waters they steamed through.

Her presence here was an inconvenience; the trouble the *Shark Saviour* had put them through would have cost them all money. She was sure she would be about as popular as a maggot in a half-eaten apple.

She was taken roughly by the arm. Her accoster was a man wearing oilskin pants, naked from the waist up, greased in sweat and tuna blood. Sinter didn't even try to hide her distaste. He led her across the decks, past the dolphin and turtle corpses, past crates and crates of rusting meat hooks, and dragged her up the metal stairway and through a doorway inside.

The bridge of the *Moumoku Maru* was a metal box, with wide glass viewing panes facing forwards. *So they could watch my friends drown*, Sinter thought grimly.

Six men stood at the bridge, all glowering at her with undisguised hatred. A bearded vagabond hissed right into her face to try and make her flinch. Sinter pursed her lips and blew him a kiss. It was bravado she wasn't feeling.

The only man who wasn't staring at her was standing at the helm. He had one hand lazily resting on the top of the wheel while he stared ahead. Something about him made him stand apart from his shipmates. Instead of oilskins, he wore jeans and a tattered grey T-shirt. His stubbly jaw was not stained walnut from the sun, his hair was not long and matted but short, his eyes not black but green. There was something else as well, something about the way he held himself, an athleticism that spoke of contained potential. He was a man who controlled a crew of hundreds through fear and strength of personality alone. Sinter could see instantly that the barbarian crew were not the ones she needed to be frightened of.

"What happened to my friends?" she demanded. "You killed them?"

The captain ignored her. Reaching down into a bowl alongside the instruments, he pulled out a lollipop, methodically unwrapped it, and put it into his mouth.

"The Ocean Code says you have to stop for a vessel in distress," said Sinter. "Failing to stop and help is an offence. Any country on earth would put you straight in prison."

At this the captain showed interest for the first time, taking the lolly from his mouth and speaking. "The brig," he said. His voice was soft, faintly accented, but European, not like the Asian voices of his crew. "On ships it's called a brig. The kitchen is a galley, the toilet is the head, the prison is the brig. Pays to know a bit more before you start spouting about laws and stuff." He started sucking his lolly again, eyes still on the horizon.

"Whatever. You're a murderer, and you'll be hung for what you've done."

"Hanged," the captain said matter-of-factly through his mouthful. "It's hanging. Meat is hung. A person is hanged. You sure talk a lot, for someone who don't know much."

Removing the lolly and pointing it at Sinter, he made eye contact with her for the first time. "And for that to happen, for me to be 'hung', you'd need witnesses to the crime. And all of them are at the bottom of the Big Blue." Then he turned his eyes back to the view. "Except you."

Sinter flinched. But it wasn't because of the threat hidden in the captain's words. It was because, as he'd turned towards her, she'd been able to see the other side of his neck. And there, in black monochrome, was the simple tattoo of a big cat's head.

"Panther," she said. There were over thirty species of big cat she could have tried for, but that looked the most likely. The captain snapped around towards her.

"Panther," she repeated. "You're Clan."

He stared at her with furious green eyes, challenging, as if waiting to pounce. Then he gave an order in a foreign tongue. The other crew members all looked at each other, not comprehending; then they left the bridge, leaving Sinter and the captain alone.

"What the hell are you talking about?" he hissed.

"You are Clan," Sinter said. "It makes sense. An operation like this has to be run by Clan."

"Like I said before," the captain responded, "you talk a lot, for someone who don't know much."

Sinter noticed he had a holstered pistol hanging alongside the helm. She needed to judge this very well indeed.

"I guess the Prophet has you farmed out here, taking care of business. It must suck to be still following his orders at your age." She guessed he was in his thirties, double the age of any Clan boy she'd ever seen.

"I follow no man," he answered, with real steel in his voice.

"Yeah, yeah," Sinter responded sarcastically, "we all like to think that."

With that she took a deep breath and rolled up her trouser leg to reveal her tattoo of the tiger's head. The captain looked down, uncomprehending.

"What is that supposed to prove?"

"Didn't you get the message?" Sinter asked. "The Clan has got all twenty-first century. They let girls in now. I was one of the first. Tigress. Which I guess makes us brother and sister."

"Really?" Panther did not sound even remotely convinced. "And how exactly does a Clan girl get to be riding shotgun on a boat full of bunny huggers?"

Sinter's mind was racing, making up her story as she

went, knowing one false step and it would all be over. "I'm a mole," she said. "A spy. Intel and sabotage. Gathering information about the activists, the 'bunny huggers', as you call them. But then you sank us. Nice work. Three of us have been working this case for almost a year, and you sent the other two to the bottom of the sea. The Prophet is going to be really upset." She left the threat hanging.

"OK, so first off, *sister*," he said it like a curse, "without a witness, it didn't happen, so you keep your smart words to yourself. And second . . ." he was snarling now, "I don't owe your Prophet anything."

A white knot appeared at his jaw as he clenched it tight shut, and the veins at his neck bulged with contained fury.

"When I reached age, I figured I'd be put out to pasture. Figured that was what happened to all of us." He gave a mirthless, dry laugh. "The old pony sent to retire on a farm somewhere."

Panther looked at Sinter with a poison that she could instantly tell was borne of years of bottled, putrefied hatred.

"Can't believe we all bought that. As if Clan just get a nice retirement package, a two-up two-down, wife, kids, a Labrador and a nice quiet office job somewhere."

Sinter gulped. How could she not have seen this coming? How on earth in all their time together had she and Saker never questioned what happened to Clan boys once they grew too old to be reliably manipulated?

"What happened?" she asked, her mouth dry as sandpaper.

"The same thing happens to everyone. He pumped me full of drugs and had me taken out into the woods to have my throat slit like a Christmas goose."

Sinter's blood ran cold. She'd completely misjudged everything.

"Before you call me brother, you might want to know I buried those boys in the same meadow they wanted to have as my grave. I didn't look back."

The chill spread through her whole body; there was a coldness in his eyes that made her skin crawl.

"So your Prophet owes me blood," he said, placing the lolly back in his mouth and staring straight ahead, all ice. "Yours will do."

Sinter protested, started trying to retract her story, to say who she really was, but he wasn't listening. He picked up a microphone and called back his shipmates, who clustered around her like baying hounds.

"I was thinking of having you work your passage, little Tigress," he said, "but not any more. I am the law out here. Your Prophet can't touch me, and he won't find me if you are shark food."

Then the captain simply nodded to his men, who took Sinter by the arms and dragged her back outside.

"Besides, I'm doing you a favour. At least I'll kill you quickly."

Sinter yelled out for mercy, but it was utterly futile. Five or six workers gripped her arms before tossing her up onto their shoulders like a coffin being taken to the funeral pyre. The workers crammed around her, yelling and cheering, showering her with fish guts and blood as she was borne screaming down the decks.

Finally, as they came to the main guardrail, Sinter was hoisted into the standing position. They stilled; savages before the sacrifice. She looked down. The sea seemed to be miles below, rushing past at impossible speed. In her peripheral vision she saw someone approaching with rope to bind her hands and feet. They were going to make her walk the plank!

With her mind racing, Sinter closed her eyes, and time slowed. Options flickered through her gaze as if on a touchscreen. To hit the sea from this height at this speed could be like hitting concrete. If her hands were tied, she might spin as she fell, hitting the water side on. She wouldn't survive the impact. The image of falling rewound and replayed, this time with Sinter taking a controlled leap. She needed to be under control, not thrown, with her feet together, and her body knife straight. To survive the sea she needed to be able to swim a long, long way. Those ropes were not an option.

With that, she slammed her elbow back into one of her captor's noses. As he reeled, she ripped her other arm free, and jumped.

17

In darkness lit by a thin, guttering beam, Saker rifled through the computer room, searching for something, anything that could tell him what to do. He'd come here in search of answers and had only ended up with more questions. Why had this place been abandoned? Had the Clan relocated? Who were his parents, and quite how much of his chemistry had been manipulated? How much was he a genetically modified assassin designed in a lab, and how much was he just a normal boy who'd been . . . well, optimised?

The paper files held nothing of interest, but that wasn't unusual. Surely everything of value would now be held on the computer drives, and those would have been wiped before the place was deserted? Even if there had been power down here, he didn't have anything like the computer skills to be able to hack into any of these machines. It was yet another dead end.

Then there was a *clump* noise, followed by a whirr and the sound of generators firing and long dead electrical systems flooding with power. The computer screens in front of him flickered into life and starting booting up. The lights above him blinked, once, twice and then were on full. Someone was here! They had tracked him already! He looked around frantically to try and find something to use as a weapon and for anything useful he could take with him if he managed to flee.

But it was already too late. He could hear the lift kicking into motion, then there was a rattling as someone stepped into the swinging cage and it started to descend. He was cornered, trapped like the rat that had led him here. And all he had to defend himself was textbooks and computer keyboards. The lift came to a halt with a clang. Saker stepped behind the door, a pathetic hiding place that could surely only buy him a few seconds.

Stealthy footsteps echoed along the corridor then the door swung open and a young man entered. He was taller than Saker, a good two years older, thicker set in the shoulders and with hair down to his shoulders; yet, somehow, the way he moved and held himself marked him as unmistakably Clan.

Saker had to assess and think fast. His mind switched into analysis mode. *The enemy is light on his feet, agile, probably with a similar totem animal to my own. Another raptor, perhaps. Two years ago he would have been my equal, and this would have been an evenly matched, fair fight. But he has had time to grow stronger, more experienced, tougher. This is a fight I cannot win on even terms.*

Right then, Saker thought, setting his jaw firm. *It can't be on level ground: it needs to be dirty.*

He had no problem with fighting dirty. There was no sense entering a clean battle he could only lose. Saker thought back to how he himself had acted upon coming into the room, reasoning his adversary would probably be attracted by the same things.

Where did I go? he thought, then remembered. *The first computer screen.*

As if he'd been instructed, the older boy did exactly what Saker had done, wandering over to the computer, his back turned to the door. Frantically looking around, Saker's eyes lit upon a red metal fire extinguisher. That would work perfectly.

The older boy was on his guard, eyes soaking in the room as if this was also his first time here. He wore jeans with training shoes, and a long-sleeved white T-shirt. Though it was quite baggy, between the shoulders and neck it pulled tight over bulging trapezius muscles. His hands looked as though they were an art project made out of walnuts and teak, and they swung from his arms as if they were genuinely heavy.

There was no sense taking any risks. As the boy stooped to look at the computer screen, Saker took his chance. Turning the fire extinguisher towards his new foe, he pulled the pin and fired it off. A blast cloud of white smoke

133

erupted from the funnel and engulfed him. Like a squid blasting a cloud of ink in front of him, the smoke would befuddle, discombobulate and confuse, whilst hiding Saker's presence – giving him the chance to attack or flee.

No more than a second after the blast, Saker followed the smoke with a leaping kick, making solid contact into the boy's chest. It was a perfectly executed move that would have dropped most combatants, but the boy stumbled backwards and kept his footing. Saker swept upwards with a knife hand aimed towards his opponent's larynx.

It was a classic sucker punch, and should have collapsed his windpipe, taking his breath, rendering him helpless. Instead, Saker's fingers were swatted away as easily as a mosquito. His nameless opponent's leg appeared out of the smoke, swinging baseball bat straight. It caught Saker in the solar plexus. An invisible force picked him up and tossed him over the computer desks. He crashed to the floor, clutching his stomach, unable to draw air into his lungs. He might as well have been kicked by an Andalucian stallion.

How was that much power even possible? As he staggered to his feet, still holding his stomach, the other boy walked round the desks, as if he had all the time in the world. Saker swung upwards with a conventional upper cut, but his foe anticipated him. He took Saker's hand and pulled it away from Saker's body, bringing him to his feet, then stepped and turned, using exquisite Aikido moves, as if leading Saker in a waltz he didn't want to dance. Saker's arm was now twisted up behind his back, and then the force came on again, thundering Saker headfirst into the filing cabinets.

Before the lights went out, he saw the dent his head had made in the metal cabinets. *Wow, that is really going to hurt when I wake up*, he thought, as colours faded to black.

It could have been hours or minutes, but when Saker came round, it did hurt. A lot. For a second there were stars whirling around his head.

I thought that only happened in cartoons, he thought to himself, now aware of a sickening pain in his head. Not surprising, as he had basically been in a head-on collision with a filing cabinet, using his face as a brake. Tenderly looking around, he saw a familiar sight: the room from his nightmare – the operating theatre, with the huge light shining down into his eyes. He looked down. The leather belt was strapped around him. The cuffs were around his wrists. He was strapped into the operating table.

"You've got to be kidding me," he whispered. For the second time in days he was in this situation – except this time it wasn't intentional. And there was no elaborate phoney virus escape plan. And he knew his unknown adversary would never fall for something so hokey. The time for trying to get the upper hand was through.

"Who are you?" he asked. Silence. That was not good. He would almost rather that there was a terrible torturer out there. Even being tortured would be better than being left here until one of the rats started to get hungry.

"Who do you think I am?" a voice boomed back from beyond his gaze.

"You are Clan," Saker responded. "I would guess your totem is a bird of prey. Though I've never seen a Clan member of your age before." That was true. Clan boys always disappeared at around sixteen years of age. This boy was on the brink of adulthood, at least eighteen.

"Did you ever wonder why?" The voice was emotionless, cold, without accent.

Saker paused. "I've often thought about it. I guess we always imagined that once the boys got too old, they were taken to the next level. A private army, perhaps?"

"Not bad – and yes, some of the more credulous boys go that way."

"But not everyone?" Saker questioned.

"No, not everyone."

"Not you?" Saker asked.

There was no answer. Then suddenly the boy was at his side. He looked long and hard at Saker, then raised his shirt and turned slightly towards him. On his lower back was a monochrome tattoo. Saker half smiled. He had at least got that bit right. The boy's tattoo was not merely the head of a bird, like Saker's own totem mark. It was a whole bird in silhouette, wings closed towards its sides, dropping out of the heavens in the dive known as a stoop.

"Peregrine," Saker said. The boy nodded. "Fastest creature ever to have lived."

The boy didn't respond to that. For anyone Clan, there was so much to be understood from the sign of one of their own. It told them pretty much everything they needed to know.

"Some of the Clan boys do go onto other assignments when they reach age," Peregrine explained, "but too many of us get wise. We get to thinking a bit too much about what it is we are doing."

Saker nodded again. Of course! There was no way he could be the only one this had happened to.

"That's when they start using the plasters," Saker chipped in. The boy looked at him with interest, cocking his head to one side as he did so. Saker could have laughed out loud; it was the exact same head movement he used himself when he was thinking about something. The head tilt of a falcon engaging its superior depth perception.

"You know about that?" Peregrine demanded.

"Of course," Saker added eagerly. "They used one on me. It seeps drugs into your system to keep you under control, but as soon as you take it off, it's all over."

"Well you don't usually wear them for long," Peregrine said. "Normally, after a few days or so, it's time for you to be decommissioned."

"Decommissioned?" Saker questioned.

Peregrine shut his eyes, clearly remembering something truly painful, and gestured to the bed Saker was lying on. "Clan members lie on this slab two times in their lives. Once when they're just a few years old and getting their assignment. And then when it's time for their final mission."

Saker understood instantly. "They execute Clan boys when they get too old."

"Of course they do!" Peregrine was almost triumphant. "They can't have highly trained criminals like us wandering around with free will! As soon as Clan boys realise that their whole lives have been building towards something evil, some of them are going to want to tear the whole thing down. And we've been trained since we could crawl to tear things apart. One of us on the loose is a nightmare. Two or three could bring the system to its knees."

The pair of them waited in silence for the implications of that to sink in.

"How did you get away?" Saker asked.

"It wasn't easy," Peregrine responded. "I had been starting to question things for a few months, but thankfully never said anything out loud. Finally I got my plaster, but a few days later I was swimming in the sea, and it washed off. I couldn't find it again, and thought I'd be in big trouble, so I replaced it with an ordinary one the same size. The next morning I woke up to a whole new world."

Saker nodded. So much of this was familiar to him, and mirrored his own story.

"It was pretty much the same for me. I never thought that a few days later it would have been . . ."

"Termination," Peregrine finished for him.

Saker nodded, a sickened realisation. He suddenly saw an image of himself on this same operating table, but the theatre bustling with white-gowned surgeons, their faces covered, brandishing lethal syringes. That was not how he wanted to go.

"And after you started to realise what was going on, then they brought you here?" Saker asked.

"Not here," Peregrine corrected, "but somewhere just like it. I gave them the slip, and they've been chasing me ever since."

The next silence was one loaded with questions. Both had so much they wanted to ask. But the explosive reality was there in plain sight. An ally! Someone who had been through the same trauma, made the same decisions, even come here at the same time. The exact same time. Wasn't that just the most ridiculous coincidence?

"Why now?" Saker started. "Why are you here now?"

Peregrine looked at him keenly, his head cocked to one side again. "What do you mean?"

"They've brought us both here together!" Saker shouted. "They've put us down here in a fortified tomb we could never escape from! You have to set me loose, it's a trap!"

With that he started to battle in his constraints, but was brought up short by a new voice. A voice that had Peregrine spinning round, hands coming up to his face in defensive stance. A voice they both knew too, too well.

"Not so much a trap," Wolf said, "more a meeting of minds."

18

Sinter choked, coughing up yet another bitter mouthful of sour saltwater. This was getting to be a habit. So thirsty . . . her lips were cracked and blistered, her cheeks raw and bloodied from abrasions and sunburn. Every single part of her body hurt, from endless hours of swimming, from the impact as she'd hit the water. But her world was no longer going up and down. In fact her face was pressed into something solid and gritty, like sand.

It was sand! She was lying face-first down in the shallows of a sandy beach, foam lapping over her. Pulling her sodden, sand-peppered hair from the swell, she levered herself up onto one elbow. She winced. It hadn't been an exaggeration, literally everything hurt. Gingerly getting to her feet, she surveyed the beach. It was immediately obvious she wouldn't merely be wandering up to a beachside hotel for a cold drink and a Band-Aid. The sands ran for less than a hundred metres in either direction before curving round again. Above the beach were palm trees and short, scrubby vegetation. There was no sign of any human being whatsoever.

"Great," Sinter said out loud through her bleeding lips. "I'm castaway on a desert island. Of course I am."

It took Sinter all of fifteen minutes to walk completely around her new home, and to find there wasn't the vaguest hint that a human being had been there before. There were various bits of plastic at the strandline where the high tide dumped them, but they were merely flotsam and jetsam, dumped into the sea and cast away here by the tide, just as she had been.

By the time she was back at the start, she felt impossibly weak and was near collapse. Her first burning need was fluids. She hadn't drunk water in many hours, and was parched by the burning sun and tropical sea. Without food she could last for more than a week. Without water she might not make nightfall. There was clearly no running water on her island, and the sky was completely clear of clouds so there was no hope of rain anytime soon.

Coconut water had been a staple drink back on the tea plantation where she had grown up, and she had seen the workers decapitating them with a machete as if it was the easiest thing in the world. But she didn't have a machete. In extreme situations, she had seen them merely smashing the nuts against the tree trunk. Well, this was certainly an extreme situation! There was no question of her climbing a tree in her condition though, so even getting a nut would be a challenge.

There were some around the base of the trees, but most were old and turning brown. She knew the milk inside would likely be fermented and wouldn't help her, making her sick.

Most of the palms towered intimidatingly high, but one was only about twice her height. It was still too big for her to climb, but had one palm branch dead, dry, brown and hanging down to within her reach. She grabbed it, shook it hard and eventually it came down, bringing down three coconuts as it fell. Sinter picked up the most likely one and, with all her power, smashed it against the tree trunk.

And nearly broke her wrist . . . but didn't put even a dent into the big green nut. There in her hands was all she needed to slake her hideous thirst. All that stood between her and that precious liquid was a few centimetres of pulp and skin. She smashed and smashed and smashed again, until her hands were raw and bleeding, and there was simply nothing left in her sinews. Dropping to her knees, she cried tears of frustration and rage. She was about to die of thirst, with her hands full of coconut water.

"Come on, Sinter," she admonished herself, "get a grip. Brains not brawn."

The rounder coconuts were no use. Her force was being evenly dissipated around the spongy shell. Taking the smallest nut in her hand, she turned it around. This one was not completely curvy, but had a pronounced edge running down it.

Sinter took it in both hands, and smashed the edge against the tree trunk. It burst instantly, spraying her face with precious drops of liquid. Sinter pressed the coconut to her face and guzzled as much as she could through the fibrous pulp, before lifting it above her head and sucking the last few drops into her mouth. It wasn't much, but it would have to do for now. It would be dark soon, and she needed a plan, not least of which was making sure she had somewhere safe to sleep.

The island, it turned out, was a classic coral atoll, circular in shape, with sand running all the way around it, and shallow waters running out to a fringing coral reef, perhaps fifty metres offshore. She could see to the horizon in every direction, and there was no sign of another island, or a passing boat coming to help.

Sinter cleared a flat area in amongst the palm trees, and then collected up as many of the fallen palm fronds as possible. Plaiting the fronds together, she interwove a simple sheet that she then propped up into a shelter. It wouldn't keep off much rain in a storm, but for now she was more worried about sun and heatstroke.

The next concern was rescue. No one knew she was lost. Even the *Shark Saviour* must surely think her dead, so no one would approach the island unless she could signal them. A fire was out. She had never learned how to light a fire without matches. Besides, she'd seen enough survival programmes to know that it wasn't as easy as you might expect. She had nothing in her pockets, no shoes, no knife. Everything she would need to survive had to come from the island itself.

The strandline was to be her hardware store. For the next few hours, Sinter walked around the high tide mark, picking through the bleached chunks of coral, driftwood and dried up seaweed to find jettisoned plastic treasures. Normally she would have been horrified by the amount of junk humans discard into our oceans, but today, she knew that it save her life. The first items of use were plastic bottles, floating in our oceans in their billions, never breaking down, here for eternity. She removed the lids, and placed them all in lines in the sand. With wrapped up funnels of palm in each mouth, they would collect rainwater. If it ever rained.

Plastic wraps that are used to contain multi-packs of soft drinks are one of the great evils in the ocean. Chucked out as litter, they eventually wash out into the ocean and are unbreakable. They snare and kill seabirds, seals and turtles. This, however, was one of the only times they would prove of any use. Sinter wrapped some sodden pieces of cloth around each foot, and then slipped the plastic wraps over the top like foot bracelets, creating passable shoes. There were lumps of tar-like oil from boat engines, which she collected with no clear idea of what they could be for. Balls of fishing line and net were gathered in case her stay ended up being a long one. They also provided a useful twine for binding the palm fronds of her shelter tightly together.

Another exciting find was an old tin lid – this would make a good knife.

It wasn't merely human junk in amongst the detritus. There were natural wonders too. Sinter found shells with glorious mother of pearl inlay, some of which held shy hermit crabs. There were small nuts that had clearly been borne over miles of ocean and had washed up here in this forgotten place, only to sprout a shoot. Pioneers, trying to settle a foreign land.

And then a dark brown leathery pouch, with spiralling wires at each corner. When Sinter held it up to the light she gasped in wonder. Silhouetted against the brown was the shape of a tiny creature within, wriggling away. It was a baby shark, and this was a mermaid's purse – the egg case it would grow in. Sinter took it back to the sea and tossed it into the surf. That was no way for a shark to die.

The best prize, though, was hidden beneath a lump of dried up seaweed high above the beach. Sinter's breath caught for a millisecond as she shifted the weed, and saw a silvery glint beneath it. At second glance, it wasn't precious metal, but a dime a dozen old CD. However, this was far more valuable than gold or platinum; it would make a superb signalling mirror should a boat get within a few miles of the island.

"Shame I haven't got anything to play it on, I could use a singsong," Sinter said to herself, before adding, "Great,

I'm talking to myself already. It didn't take long for me to go loco."

The last find of the day, though, choked the brave humour from her lips. She found a cheap plastic toy of an Indian girl. She was dancing barefoot, posed with her palms raised, dressed in a sari swirling around her legs that had once been red but was now bleached pink by the sun. It was nothing special, a cheap toy given away with a Happy Meal, tossed into the garbage and washed out to sea. But somehow it took Sinter home.

Home to the plantation, where the black-eyed girls plucked tea, with their vibrant saris and gold nose rings. Where she had her bath drawn for her by her own nurse, where aromatic scents of cardamom and jasmine drifted beneath the ceiling fans. Back before her father had betrayed her. The world she kept now only in a locket with a faded image of her long dead mother.

A guttural sob left her body, and she drew her arm back in fury and threw the plastic doll off into the surf before turning away, shamed at her own tears. Then she was gripped by remorse. Maybe it was as simple as her deep hatred of throwing garbage into the sea, maybe it was something more profound. Whichever, she stumbled down the sand into the swell, and started groping around for the discarded doll. It bobbed to the surface and she grabbed it, clasping it to her chest with a relief she didn't understand.

*

As the day faded, the sun became a massive blood orange which drained into the sea, staining the sky red. The heat left the day, and Sinter walked around her island, scanning the horizon for a ship that didn't come. Eventually it started to get dark. Sinter whacked her way into another coconut, then laid down in the sand beneath her shelter. Looking up at the faded doll above her bed, Sinter said goodnight.

"You've floated your way around the world," she told the plastic dancer, "never letting life sink you, and you ended up here. You're a fighter, little plastic dancer."

"We have a lot in common, you and I." She smiled. "We should be pals."

19

*J*ust *let me free of these cuffs*, Saker thought to himself, *and I'll tear you limb from limb, you lying mutt.*

Peregrine had taken to pacing the room, head and hands twitching as nervously as his namesake, as if so packed with nervous energy and hyper-stimulated by overdeveloped senses that they simply could not stay still.

Why isn't he doing anything? Saker thought. *Peregrine could kill Wolf and let us out of this godforsaken place.*

"So what gives, Wolf?" Peregrine eventually asked. "Why the change of heart so suddenly?"

Saker agreed. "You've always been the Prophet's pet puppy. How do you expect us to believe you're all of a sudden the big rebel?"

Wolf chewed on his lip and nodded a sort of agreement. "I got one thing from my namesake," he said. "One thing wolves excel at is survival."

And then he added, "A wolf will chew off its own leg

148

to escape from a leg-hold trap. I knew I was dead if I tried to escape. And I knew what I had to do to stay alive."

"So you just ignored it all?" Saker asked. "All that killing, the crazy stuff we were made to do? What made you change your mind?"

"What was it made *you* change *your* mind?" Wolf fired back. "Was there any one moment, or was it just a lifetime of drips on your face that finally woke you up?"

Saker pondered his words. He wasn't even sure. It almost seemed as though life had begun in the forests of India, with the tigress he'd brought down with an arrow. With the feeling that he was doing something deeply wrong, with the sense that he had taken the life of a sacred animal.

"It was the tiger, wasn't it?" asked Wolf. "Being party to the death of an animal we were being asked to admire? It suddenly all felt wrong, didn't it?"

Both Saker and Peregrine looked at Wolf with a growing awareness.

"Well, it was the same for me," Wolf said. "The Prophet sent me on a mission to the Arctic where some trash redneck was killing wolves to order. I mean, seriously? I *am* a wolf! Every pelt I saw felt like murder, like they were murdering one of my own. Of course I saw what was going on, and I needed a way out. I thought that way out was killing you, and proving I was loyal."

He drew breath, spit flecking his cheeks as he spoke, a passion Saker had only ever seen when Wolf was hunting.

"But eventually I knew I'd reached the end. No matter what happened, whether I found you or lost you, I was coming back to be decommissioned."

He looked down and drew a deep breath. "It was time to choose a side. I chose my own. And that means choosing you two. Don't get too flattered – the alternative was a shallow grave."

The following minutes were silent, except for the sounds of clicking cogs in the brains of Saker and Peregrine.

Eventually Peregrine spoke. "So what now? The Clan will hunt us till we're all in that same shallow grave."

"I've spent two years trying to disappear," added Saker. "They always find me."

"We can't run any more," Wolf stated, the old steel back in his voice.

"And I can't continue to let them do the things they've done," Saker said through clenched teeth.

Wolf walked up to the operating table, and there was the sound of a dagger being scraped from out of its sheath. Saker gasped as he saw a glint of light on razor-edged steel. But then the cuffs sprang apart, like chocolate sliced with a hot scalpel. Saker pulled his hands free, swung himself off the table and was standing, hands clenched, ready for a fight.

Wolf stood in front of him, square on, defensive posture, knife gripped ready for a slashing underhand blow to the stomach. Gold eyes met black; they may as well have snarled like dogs ready to be unleashed. But then Wolf relaxed his posture. He loosened his grip on the knife, which swung between thumb and forefinger. Slowly and carefully, he placed the knife down on the operating table between the two of them. And then, very deliberately, he turned away from Saker, offering up his back. Saker snatched the knife in his hand, taking a classic fatal stabbing grip.

"Strikes me that what we need to do is to break the Clan from inside," said Wolf, "and I know just how to do it."

Seconds seemed like hours. Wolf stood offering his back to Saker's blade, a clear and cataclysmic gesture of trust, challenging Saker to stab him between the shoulder blades. Peregrine's eyes flicked between them as if he was tracking a pigeon on the wing.

"Do you still have that phone you took from me?" Wolf asked. Saker thought he sensed a tremor in Wolf's voice. A tiny droplet of sweat trickled down the side of his face. Wolf was scared too. Saker exhaled, shook his head at the madness of it all, and placed the knife back on the table.

"Of course I do. It won't work down here though," Saker said, fishing the phone out of his pocket and passing it over. Wolf turned back around. Saker could see the beads of sweat on his forehead as he passed him the phone.

Wolf took it with evident relief. "Just as well. I wouldn't use this above ground – it tracks our every move to within a few square metres. If things go wrong, the Prophet could call in a team in minutes."

Saker had a jolt of recollection. He'd turned the phone

on in the forest to get his GPS co-ordinates. There could be an unpleasant surprise waiting for them when they returned to the surface. When would be the appropriate time to mention he'd already used it?

Wolf laid the phone down on the table. Pressing his thumb on the scan button, the unique pattern of his fingerprint was scanned. The home screen changed. It was no longer the default background that Saker had seen when he used the phone to check his location. It briefly showed an image of Wolf's totem tattoo before a new, secret, section of the phone opened, showing a pattern of hieroglyphic options. There were no flash graphics, just simple symbols.

Wolf pressed one of the hieroglyphs. It flashed once or twice, then projected beams up into the air. Wolf went to the wall and turned off the lights, then wiped his palms over one of the dusty monitor screens. He then clapped his hands over the phone. The blue-green light from the phone caught the dust particles in the air and illuminated a moving hologram.

Saker and Peregrine gasped. It was the three-dimensional face of the Prophet. Then sound erupted from the speaker as he began talking.

"I need you to eradicate this problem. It has become too *troublesome* . . ."

Saker shuddered. It was that familiar method of over-emphasising some words that set the Prophet's speech patterns apart.

"You will travel to the Crimea, to the Minsk Quarter station. He is there. I want him returned alive if possible. If not, then end him. And then you will return for your punishment. I will not look favourably on another failure."

All three caught their breath. Even in a trick projection, the Prophet had the power to reduce them all to frightened little boys. The power of fear he had over them made the surgery suddenly feel as cold as an abattoir.

"What is this?" Peregrine asked.

"The Clan has finally decided to get with the times," answered Wolf. "The last few years, smartphones and computer hacking have been as much a part of our training as fighting and fitness." He turned to Saker. "We have your Vietnamese friend to thank for that."

Saker sniggered. His Vietnamese friend was Minh, a socially inept teenager with a penchant for illegal hacking, who had outwitted the whole Clan with a laptop and an internet connection.

"The phones track us and our movements," Wolf continued, "but they're also used to deliver our missions, and to keep us under control."

Wolf explained, "These little devices have become the centre of our world. Without them we have no direction, no mission. And because of the security, we trust them. We'll do whatever they tell us to."

Peregrine was starting to nod, and Saker too could see the potential in the slim bit of hi-tech.

"These phones may have taken us into the future, but

the Prophet doesn't really understand technology," Wolf went on.

Saker nodded his agreement; the Prophet had always been pretty old school.

"So they could be the Clan's Achilles heel," Peregrine ventured.

"Exactly," Wolf agreed, "and I think your Vietnamese friend could be just what we need."

20

It had been a sleepless night. The tropical beach had been paradise at sunset, but was decidedly chilly at two in the morning, and Sinter had ended up pulling sand over herself in a futile attempt to stem the cold. A short rainstorm had added to the misery, and she'd been glad of the paltry shelter provided by her palm fronds. Biting bugs had been whining around her ears all night long, and just as she was dropping off to sleep a big rat ran over her feet, making her jump.

It felt like a mixed blessing then, as the sun finally began to rise on the other side of the island, the sky turning light pink and powder-blue. Sinter yawned and rolled over to come face to face with the Plastic Princess.

"I'm guessing you slept better than I did?" she asked. The dancer stared back at her with her bleached-out eyes.

"Not bringing much to the party really, are you?"

Still the same blank smile.

"OK, OK, shut up already, you never stop talking do you? Can't get a word in edgeways!"

Sinter shivered for a few minutes more, before the sun properly came up. For half an hour after the dawn the temperature was blissful, and it seemed that this place could be paradise after all . . . before the burning heat began again, sending Sinter scurrying for the shade.

The shower in the night had half filled all of her water bottles, which meant she could properly slake her thirst for the first time, and even wash the encrusted salt off her face. But now that she was no longer so thirsty, the hunger pangs began to gnaw in her stomach. Her tin lid knife was not robust enough for cutting into the coconuts, and much as she would have liked to catch and cook her rat, this didn't seem to be a realistic plan. It was going to have to be the sea that provided.

The tide was at its highest, so Sinter gathered some rocks up and built a wall in a circular shape, with an opening at one end. In the centre, she placed a dead, rotting fish she'd found up at the strandline. An hour or so later, when she peered cautiously into the trap, there were already a few small fish darting inside to nibble at the stinky, rotten bait. Later in the morning, as the tide started to recede, she completed the wall with a few more rocks, trapping several decent-sized fish inside.

Raw, wriggling, slimy fish were thoroughly unappetising, but Sinter was starving and, without a fire to cook them, she had no other choice. Taking one by the tail, she smashed its head on a rock to kill it, and then took her tin lid and sliced out the entrails. It took all of her will power to bite into the flesh, but she just kept saying to herself: "It's only sushi, it's only sushi."

As she sucked the last meat off the bones, she felt the protein surging through her body and felt a little strength returning. But if she was honest, it didn't do much to ease her hunger. It had only been a day shipwrecked and she was exhausted, had no idea how to make fire and had a permanent grizzling hunger pain in her stomach.

If she'd only known how well she was doing, and that thousands of survivalists could not have matched her achievements, she might well have just stayed in her shelter and snoozed for the afternoon. Instead, she picked up the palm fronds as a parasol to keep off the sun, and started to walk the strandline again.

There was nothing much of interest: a few more plastic bottles to add to the collection, another rag that she tied over her head as a sun hat. But then her eye was caught by a glint beneath a mat of drying seagrass. She pulled it aside, and gasped. It was a glass jar, missing a lid, but with a thick bottom to it like a magnifying glass.

Sinter could barely wait to try out her new discovery and, ripping some fibres from off the nearest palm, she squatted down with the top of the jar pointed towards the sun and the bottom pointed towards the tinder. Sinter moved the jar backwards and forwards, focusing the circle of sunlight onto the dry fibres. When the circle was at its smallest and most intense, Sinter held her concentration, and waited.

It seemed she waited for an eternity. Perhaps an hour went past with nothing at all. She was drenched with sweat from just sitting there holding the same position. Perhaps the tinder wasn't dry enough. Maybe the glass didn't make an effective enough magnifying glass. It just wasn't working. But then she jumped with delight. A rising, thin, whisper of smoke! Just the tiniest, thinnest suggestion, but smoke nonetheless.

She held the jar without wavering, muscles aching, and the frond started to smoulder, the edges of the white dot of sunlight glowing faint red as the fibres took light. She blew on them gently as they started to spread. And then suddenly, the frond leapt into flame. Sinter squealed with excitement and joy. She placed the fledgling fire down on the ground, and fed in some more palm fibres. They disappeared in seconds. Frantically, she jumped up to try and find more fuel, but there was nothing nearby. Tearing down to the beach, she scrabbled around for some kindling, but by the time she returned, just seconds later, the fire was reduced to smoking ashes. It was dead. Sinter could have cried.

"The secret to success is prior planning and preparation," she told the plastic dancer seriously. "Saker would be furious with me."

The next two hours was spent gathering dry fibres from

coconut husks and paper-like slices of bark, and stacking all the spare branches, driftwood and dried brown palm she could find. She put them all into organised piles according to size next to her shelter. Then taking the finest fibres as tinder and the lumps of tar as an accelerant, she set to work.

"This time we're ready," she told Plastic Princess.

Minutes ticked by, but eventually a tiny plume grew from the tinder. Blowing gently at the base of it, she saw orange start to glow. Then with an audible puff, a flame! She shrieked with delight.

Just half an hour later, Sinter was adding fuel to her fire. Fire, the thing that sets us aside from our animal counterparts. Fire, that since the dawn of time has been one of the greatest advances for humankind. Fire, that transforms life in the outdoors, and turns a survival situation into a camping trip.

Sat staring into the dancing sprites of her fire, for the first time, Sinter knew she was going to be all right.

But with every level of survival, a new foe raises its head. When you sort out your thirst, you realise you are hungry. When you sort your hunger, then it's the need for a roof over your head. Once that's done, it's fire. Once you have fire and cooked food, and don't have to think about surviving every second . . . then the wider world starts to intrude.

For the first time, she realised with a pang of shame that she hadn't thought about Mistral or the rest of the boat crew since she was on the *Moumoku Maru*. It seemed certain they had all perished, but there was still some hope. If she had managed to swim to safety, then there was a slim chance they could have done the same. Maybe the *Shark Saviour* did know she was lost? Maybe they were out looking for her after all?

"That's just crazy talk," she told Plastic Princess. "Thinking like that can drive you nuts."

And then she looked again at the doll.

"Nuts enough to end up having a conversation with an Indian Barbie doll."

She sighed and rolled her other side to the fire. The sun had set on her second day, and the air was starting to chill again. A big chunk of driftwood on the fire would hopefully make sure the pre-dawn chill wouldn't keep her awake again.

"Night night, Plastic Princess," she said. "Don't keep me up all night with your dancing and partying. I need my beauty sleep."

And with that, she rolled over and slipped into a sleep filled with dreams of sea monsters and faded toys that came to life. Of drowning friends, Arctic wolves and avalanches. But however distressing the dreams were, they only flittered around her brain before flying away, and she slept soundly till the first rays of dawn fell on her sleeping face.

21

The swinging elevator bucket chugged its way upwards under the weight of the three boys, small lights at regular intervals illuminating the shaft, which was rough-hewn out of the rock itself. *So that's what it looks like,* Saker thought, as they headed slowly back to ground level.

"Errrrmm . . . I'm not sure if now would be a good time to mention this," he said, as the two others looked at him, "but I might have turned the phone on. Before. When I was outside."

Wolf closed his eyes and looked to the ceiling.

"Perfect," Peregrine hissed.

"I didn't know!" Saker protested. "It was only to use the GPS to find this place – I mean, it was only switched on for a few minutes. Maybe they haven't found us yet?"

"They'll have picked it up," Wolf said with resignation,

"no doubt about that. It just depends whether they've had time to mobilise."

"And if they've got anyone in the area," Peregrine reasoned. "This place has been shut down for months – they might not have any Clan nearby."

"Maybe not, but this is the twenty-first century," Wolf said. "There are other terrors than just the Clan."

"So we head out together," Wolf said. "Anything we find, we take on as a team. If we need to split up, meet in two days at recce point Majestic."

Saker racked through his brains to his training. *Majestic?* Yes, he remembered.

On reaching the exit, the boys stood for a second and looked at each other one last time. Then they nodded, and ran outside into the gully.

As Saker sprinted down the rocky alleyway, a whirring sound shot overhead, as if someone had thrown a high-powered desk fan through the air. There was a peashooter sound and something whistled past his cheek before rattling onto the ground. He glanced down as he ran. It was a dart, but the main shaft was a plastic vial, with pink-feathered flights. He'd seen these before, used to deliver potentially lethal poison into Sinter when they were up in the Arctic.

"Drones!" Wolf shouted.

Saker risked a look upwards. A squadron of plastic quadro-copters the size of dustbin lids zoomed over like alien spaceships, small gyro-stabilised cameras hanging beneath, twisted to focus on him. A volley of shots rang out, and the air was filled with poison darts. Saker dived out of the gully, hearing the vials ping harmlessly off the rock.

Peregrine came charging past him. Wolf danced ahead through the bracken. The drones banked, their copter blades whirring – lifeless, empty, plastic bodies shining white in the beams of light cutting down through the pine canopy high above. Saker reached down to his feet, picking up a baseball-sized rock, then drew back his arm and threw. The projectile smashed into one of the drones, clattering it sideways. It bounced to the ground, plastic parts and pieces popping off in every direction, blades chopping uselessly into the pine needles. Suddenly it transformed from a lethal killing machine into a discarded Christmas toy, broken by Boxing Day.

"Good shot," Peregrine exclaimed, gripping Saker by the collar and wrenching him to his feet. The three moved now into a loose arrowhead formation, travelling erratically through the undergrowth as if ordered by some secret master. Only Wolf had been specifically prepared to avoid drones like these, but in many ways this was similar to what they had all trained for, evading snipers' arrows and bullets. They ran with erratic gaits, leaping from side to side, making it impossible for the drones to focus on them and predict their trajectory.

Peregrine hammered through chest-high ferns, dropping with one hand to scoop up a fallen branch. Then with exquisite, almost ballerina-like grace, he swayed sideways and spun on one foot, sweeping the branch around as he went, with the aim and impetus of an Olympic hammer thrower. The end of the branch clouted a drone, smashing it into tiny pieces. The guttering remnants spun out of control and burst – cogs, batteries, wires and motors popping onto the forest floor.

Saker was about to whoop his encouragement, but had to duck as he was nearly decapitated by a zigzagging copter. Dropping into a forward roll he came back to his feet and sprinted on, deliberately splintering from the other two boys. The drones could no longer follow all three of them and the hesitation as the operators chose who to pursue could be the chance they needed.

This was their world, the environment where they felt most at home. The Clan had trained them in these forests from birth to be perfect predators, and their feet danced as easily here as the deer's and the fox's. Technology was no match for their pure, natural ease with the place. He risked a glance over his shoulder.

"You've got to be kidding me!" he hissed, seeing one hot on his heels. "What's wrong with the other two?"

Saker's stride lengthened as he covered a flat section, drawing the drone towards him. Although he was accustomed to being the hunter, this time he was the hunted, and he needed to adapt his plan. This was the strategy prey animals adopt when being pursued by faster, less manoeuvrable predators, and exactly why sheep run on ahead of your car when you're in the countryside, only dodging to the side when you are practically upon them. It's inherent evasive behaviour – dodge too soon and the predator has time to adjust and will surely make the kill. Dodge at the last millisecond and leave them snapping at air, sprawling in the dust as their prey makes a tight turn.

Saker slowed, hearing the drone gaining, hearing the dart turret whirring, readying itself to fire. But as the first dart clicked into the breech, he threw a huge sidestep, stopping dead and allowing the drone to fly right past. Saker then dropped flat on his stomach in the bracken. With its four whirring blades, the drone was far faster than him in flat out speed, but nowhere near as quick to stop.

Seconds later he chanced a glance upwards. The drone was hovering just ahead of him, twirling from side to side, the under-slung camera sweeping around. Saker could just imagine the frantic remote operator – possibly miles away, even on a different continent, scanning the images, desperate to find him. Then the camera clunked, refocused, and turned to stare at Saker.

He couldn't have known, but the remote operator had flicked a switch that turned the camera from normal vision to thermal, picking up heat and warmth rather than light. Even though Saker was hidden in the bracken, his heat signature glowed against the cool ground, making him instantly visible. The dart turret swung round to focus on him again and, cursing technology, Saker leapt to his feet and ran once more. This time he dodged, hoping to prevent the drone locking on to him. As it gained, he stumbled, staggering to his hands like a monkey. As he came upright the drone was right on top of him. Pure instinct led him to snatch out at the droid as it spun past, catching it by one of the struts on the base. Now he suddenly found himself battling with a furious beast, the camera spinning to try and focus on Saker. The camera whirred on its gyro and came to face him, then so too did the peashooter-like cannon underneath, that must surely fire the lethal darts. Saker twisted away from it as the barrel unloaded a volley of darts, one after the other. The lethal projectiles whizzed past his ear until the contraption sputtered, all its ammunition spent. Seeing his moment of advantage, Saker swung the drone in a wide arc, smashing it against a nearby tree trunk. It exploded into tiny pieces.

Wolf was being hotly pursued by the last drone, which was whipping low at waist height through the bracken, its copter blades slicing through the greenery like a hedge trimmer. Suddenly Wolf's feet fell away from him, and he was tumbling into a gully, sliding through loose, dry leaves, tossed by momentum over a fallen tree. As he slid onto his back at the bottom of the depression, the drone banked, stalled, and its camera focused down on its target. The cannon fired, and fired again until it ran dry of ammunition. Then, without its chief weapon, the blades re-orientated, and the copter made straight for Wolf as he edged away on his back.

The drone aimed straight for him, its whirring blades suddenly become a means of attack, directed at Wolf's throat. In slow motion he lifted his hand to deflect the oncoming automaton, but it soared on mercilessly, chopping into his forearm. Wolf yelled out in pain as the cold blades sliced his flesh and blood flew.

Then a crunch, and the whirring died. Peregrine had appeared out of nowhere, like the bird that was his namesake, smashing into the drone with his whole body, tackling it midair and bringing it to the ground. As Wolf reclined, a helpless onlooker, Peregrine raised his tree-branch weapon and obliterated the drone, smashing it into tiny pieces. The two relaxed briefly, panting to reclaim their breath. Saker slid down the bank through the dry leaves to join them.

"Is that all of them?" he gabbled.

"I think so," Peregrine responded. "But there will be more."

"And now they know we're alive, and together," said Saker, thinking back to the under-slung cameras that had been staring at him, doubtless relaying their images straight back to the Clan and the Prophet. "They'll be hunting us even harder now."

"We need to move, and move fast," Wolf said from the leaves. "We still have the advantage. As long as we can stay ahead of them, we have the edge."

He could tell from his companions' faces they didn't believe him. They were just staring at him in silent disbelief.

"What?" he asked. "Don't tell me the two of you have gone soft on me?"

"It's not that, Wolf," Peregrine said. His tone was desperate, desolate, as if all hope was gone. And both of them were staring at Wolf's neck.

Wolf stared back, uncomprehending. Then, reaching up to his neck, he found the feathers of a dart protruding. He'd been hit.

"But I didn't feel anything," Wolf complained. "I don't feel anything at all."

"The worst poisons and venoms are always that way, Wolf," Saker stated. "You know that. When you shot Sinter full of tetrodotoxin she didn't feel anything either."

"What else can you feel?" Peregrine asked. He had knelt down at Wolf's side, and calmly unbuttoned the top of Wolf's tunic, making breathing as easy as possible. Ripping the dart out and flinging it to one side, he pressed his fingers into Wolf's jugular to take his pulse.

"Well, nothing," Wolf said. "I feel fine."

But that wasn't true.

"His heart rate's gone through the roof," Peregrine said.

"Looks like ptosis too," said Saker, pointing at Wolf's eyelids, which seemed to be drooping closed against Wolf's will.

Wolf stirred. He'd heard that word before; ptosis?

Wasn't that when your eyelids started to shut without you being sleepy?

"You look all weird," Wolf said. His voice was slurred, like a drunk man.

"In what way? How do I look weird?"

"It's like . . . it's like the walls are closing in. Like my eyes are going dark from the sides."

"Tunnel vision?" Saker asked. Peregrine nodded.

"And now . . . now it's going all white, white like clouds."

"OK listen to me, this is important." Peregrine had him by the shoulders now. "What can you taste?"

Wolf looked at him as if he was mad. What could he taste? Why would he taste anything? He hadn't eaten for hours! In fact he was quite hungry – he could feel himself salivating at the thought. How odd. And the saliva, it tasted all . . . well, all . . .

"It tastes rusty," Wolf said with surprise. "Just like rusty metal."

Saker and Peregrine looked at each other in horror. Tunnel vision, ptosis, metallic taste in the mouth. They knew exactly what it was. The venom of a black mamba. The largest venomous snake in Africa, possibly the fastest in the world, and potentially one of the most dangerous. Its venom was no more than highly evolved snake saliva, yet a pinprick of it could kill a human being. Before anti-venom had been developed, a mamba bite was considered one hundred per cent fatal. Now things were not so bad, and many people survived if they were treated quickly with the antidote. But they were a long way from any anti-venom. And you might survive a single droplet, but Wolf had been injected with a vial-full.

They both knew there was no sense in trying to suck the venom out of the wound. Spreading factors in the venom meant that it would surge through the bloodstream like a drop of ink billowing in a glass of water.

"It's going to be OK, Wolf," Saker said, with a certainty he didn't feel. "We'll get you to help. You'll be back out there making my life hell by the weekend."

"Don't give me that, Saker," Wolf said calmly. "I went through the same training as you did. I know exactly what this is. And I know how this ends."

The late summer sun illuminated flecks of windborne pollen and dust from the wings of startled butterflies. A goshawk's angry clucking call sounded off in the verdant cavern. And Wolf's racing heart rate slowed beneath Peregrine's fingertips. He could count every pulse; counting Wolf's life force, slipping away.

"I can see a white light," Wolf chuckled. "The cliché is true; you really do see a white light! Perhaps I'm going to heaven." With that his laugh became strangled, bitter.

"It's the venom, Wolf, it messes with your senses," Saker whispered. "Lie back down, you'll be more comfortable."

"Comfortable for what?" Wolf stuttered. "So I can die lying on my back? For you to give me the Last Rites? There's no heaven waiting for me. I've done terrible things. You know that. I had this coming. This is justice."

"Don't say that. You were going to make things right."

"And now I'll never get the chance." His voice was strangled now. "Now I'm going to die here thanks to a poxy radio-controlled kid's toy and a couple of drops of snake spit. I'm done. But you can still finish it, Saker. You can make it right. End all this. Smash the Clan, destroy it."

With that he reached into his pocket and took out the phone, clasping it into Saker's hands as if it was some kind of sacred heirloom or keepsake. "You know what to do."

"Wolf, we can beat this," Peregrine urged. "Stick with me brother, we'll get help."

"I've had enough mamba venom to kill an elephant," Wolf countered, still lucid through the white fog that was infecting his brain. His tongue felt swollen, like a doormat in his mouth. Every word was a marathon.

"And I was finished the second I ran. I'm not strong like you, Saker."

Saker started at this, at his greatest adversary admitting defeat. To his utter shock, he saw a drop of fluid gather at the end of his own nose, and drip into the leaves. Tears were trickling down his face for the first time he could ever remember.

"Turns out I was never the Alpha after all." Wolf was weak now. "I was just a pack dog. Just a follower. Turns out I can't do anything without being given an order. But you can make a difference."

"I promise you," Saker said, "I promise. I won't rest till this is over."

"I always knew it would end here," Wolf whispered, looking up at the leaves swaying in the breeze above him. "But not like this." And with that, his eyes closed.

The goshawk called again. The wind hesitated then whispered through the leaves. The forest took a breath, as Wolf took his last.

22

Staring back from the hazy, distorting CD mirror, was a face Sinter barely recognised. After less than a week on the island, she looked gaunt and drawn from the lack of food, her skin jaundiced and papery from the scant water.

"Not that a rusty tin can makes much of a mirror," she confided to the Plastic Princess, "but I am certainly not the belle of the ball right now."

After the first few days of hell, she'd settled into a kind of routine, rising before dawn so as to get the majority of the hard work done before the heat of the day scorched her skin. She'd walk the strandline, looking for treasures that had been left there by the night's high tide, gathering driftwood for the fire and rotting marine life as bait for the fish trap. Plastic Princess was now standing on a stage constructed from a toy truck, and was joined by a rubber duck, a plastic hair-brush and a snow storm with the Taj

Mahal inside. It was another weird reminder of India, of home and her past.

In the early 1990s, a huge storm washed some packing crates off the decks of an oceangoing freighter. They were filled with little yellow plastic ducks, intended to be used as floating toys in people's bathtubs. Those rubber ducks travelled around the world for over two decades, washing up on beaches spanning the globe, and journeying as much as twenty thousand miles. Oceanographers charted their journeys and used them to help us understand how ocean currents work. They are just a fragment of the vast array of plastic castaways set adrift on our seas, caught in gyres and whirlpools for years, tainting the perfection of our biggest and wildest environment.

Much of it is formed from trash we lazily throw away on our streets, that ends up in storm drains and then gets flushed out to sea. Some slicks of plastic are the size of countries, some are eaten by marine creatures and some choke and strangle others. Despite the fact that Sinter's beach was remote and unknown, the sands were washed every day with plastic garbage that could have come from the other side of the world.

The one thing Sinter really wasn't happy with was her shelter. Building it had been way down the list after fire, food and water, and she hadn't had the opportunity to improve it much. She'd added a few more plaited palm walls to the roof, this time using green, fresh palm fronds, which were much more waterproof. She'd reinforced the ceiling with another panel so it was a bit more windproof. One side opened out onto the fire pit. On the other side of the fire she had built another palm wall, so that the heat from the fire could be reflected back towards her as she slept. Her bed was padded with coconut-palm fibres, and her pillow was a chunk of flotsam polystyrene. That had been a great find.

"Shame the tide hasn't brought me a nice duvet," she mused.

Sinter rubbed her hands into the ashy remains of the previous night's fire, and gathered some charcoal dust on her fingertips. She then proceeded to rub the black dust gently onto her teeth, cleaning them with her makeshift toothbrush. Halfway through, she stopped to admire her reflection in her tin can mirror. The resulting image had her giggling out loud.

"It gets even better – I look like a toothless witch!" she said out loud. "For minty fresh breath and teeth that shine . . . Charcoal, cos I'm worth it!"

Spitting out the black dust, she rinsed her mouth out with rainwater from one of the gathering bottles. On the second day she had carelessly knocked a bottle over, spilling the precious water into the sand. Now the bottles were always kept in deep holes in the sand. She was learning fast.

With her tooth brushing done, she organised the figurines and gewgaws on her little shelf. For some reason, their exact setting and position had become incredibly important to her, as had the schedule of her day. Food was the first big challenge.

"Breakfast is the most important meal of the day," she said solemnly to her inanimate friends. "Can't tackle anything with an empty stomach."

"So what will it be?" Sinter mused out loud. "Masala dosa? Eggs Benedict? Perhaps some spinach on the side?"

With a sardonic sigh, she instead picked up a piece of fish that she'd dried in the sun. It stank of . . . well, of rotten fish, and tasted salty and nasty, but it was protein, and would give her the energy she needed to get the day underway.

"This tastes like old boots," she confided to her plastic pals. "Actually, scratch that, it tastes like fish sick. But hey ho, beggars can't be choosers."

At the shoreline she found a green fleshy plant growing with glossy leaves – sea purslane. It was salty but not unpleasant to the taste, and after smearing some on her forearms and lips to see if it was irritating, she decided it was pretty good eating, and used it to disguise the old boot taste of the dried fish.

She'd woven a sun hat out of the old brown leaf bases of the palm, and stitched it together with twisted fishing line, using an old fish-bone to make needle holes. She put it on before setting off for the post-dawn scavenge, to keep the daytime scorch off her face. This was the most important activity of the day. What she found would determine her morale for the rest of the long day.

"Slim pickings at the strandline today," she said out loud to no one. She'd been nearly an hour wandering along the high tide mark, and found nothing of interest. Sometimes the flow gave up surprising treasures, other times it was much less charitable. Bleached white chunks of coral stood like ghost trees in amongst the shells and drying sea grass. Suddenly something stopped her in her tracks. She squinted her eyes against the fierce tropical sunshine.

Was that . . . no, it couldn't be . . . it was!

"Ship," she said quietly, disbelieving. Then louder: "Ship, it's a ship!"

The silhouette was way out at the horizon, which she knew would be about four miles away. If it turned slightly away from her, it would be out of sight in minutes. She had to act fast. Sprinting up the beach, she ran to her camp.

The fire was still smouldering – she kept it turning over with minimal fuel during the day so that she would not have to go through the process of lighting it again every evening. Now she dumped on all her most precious logs, using the palm wall of her shelter as a fan to whip the fire into flames. Then, as it started to rage, she threw on some chunks of old boat engine tar, which started to instantly spew out black smoke. Then some green palm leaves, which threw out acrid brown plumes.

The fumes burned the back of her throat, but she was too excited to care. As the twisting dark spiral made its way skywards, Sinter grabbed her CD and raced back down to the shoreline. Angling it slightly towards the sun, she caught a flash of light on the reflective plastic, and tried to flash the signal towards the ship on the horizon. She angled it to give three short flashes, then three long ones, then another three short ones – the universal Morse code for SOS: Save Our Souls.

"Come on come on!" She willed the boat to turn, to come to her rescue. "You've got to see me, surely!"

At that distance the blurry shape at the horizon was tricky to perceive, but she fancied it was coming around.

"It's turning," she said, "it's coming my way!"

This was it – rescue, she was saved. Any minute now the broadside view she had of the ship would become a head on view, and it would be bound for her little island.

"No more shoe sole suppers, no more flea-bitten beds, no more sunstroke and no more having conversations with old bits of garbage. No offence, Plastic Princess, but I'm out of here!"

Sinter ran an eye over her camp, looking for anything she definitely couldn't do without, and deciding that everything could stay. It would make a curious display should anyone come here in a few years' time, to find a tatty shelter and the sad shelf of the world's most disappointing toy shop.

But something was wrong. "That ship must be really

big," she mused. "It's taking for ever to turn this way."

Then she had a horrible thought. *Perhaps it's the* Moumoku Maru, *come back to finish me off!*

But no. The *Maru* had one funnel, set well back on the boat; this one had two. It wasn't the *Maru*. It also wasn't turning. If anything, the ship appeared to be getting more and more hazy in view, fading from sight. It hadn't seen her.

"No no no!" she yelled in frustration. "How can you not see me? I've got black smoke going up five storeys high!"

She began flashing the CD mirror now with even greater speed, frantically sending her distress signals out over the waves. But it was pointless. No one was watching. The distant silhouette faded still further, and then was gone over the horizon.

Sinter had never felt so alone in her whole life. So far from home, from everyone else on the planet. No one was coming to save her; she was going to die here on this tiny island she could walk around in fifteen minutes.

Sinter cried bitter tears into the crick-crackling remains of the fire for what seemed like the entire morning, but in reality was probably only a few minutes.

"Don't be so pathetic," she said angrily. "You're supposed to be tough. You worked damn hard to gather all that water, what's the use of crying it into the sand. Pull yourself together."

The human brain is a powerful thing. The most powerful

organ on the planet. It's astounding what wonders it can work, when fixed in the right direction.

"Come on, there's nobody going to find lunch for you. Either toughen the hell up, or go hungry – it's your choice."

It was remarkable how much better that simple statement of resolve made her feel. It would have been easy to slip into a depression and just fade away, but Sinter wasn't going to let that happen.

"Baby steps," she reminded herself. "Think routine, schedule. Even a journey of a thousand miles begins with a single step. Let's make a plan."

With her mind set on renewed positivity, Sinter wrote a shopping list in the sand for the rest of her day, and then the rest of the week.

First step, was to go diving out in the shallows, to see if she could find anything edible. Sinter found a thin spear-like stick, and used the jagged edge of her tin lid to whittle the end of it to a sharp point. This could function like a kind of harpoon. At the other end, she tied a loop of fishing line, with a slipknot so that it could tighten when pulled. She'd seen local fishermen snagging lobster like this, slipping the knot over their tails, and yanking it tight to ensnare them.

Hanging her precious sun hat on a coconut palm, she stripped down to her bathing suit, and walked with purpose down to the shoreline, weapon clasped in her hand. This would be a real challenge without goggles or fins, but she had to learn to improvise. The water was cool against her skin, and it relieved some of the heat of frustration. She started focusing on her breathing exercises, emptying her brain, dropping her heart rate, preparing to enter an alien world.

Immersed in the Blue, she closed her eyes to slits to improve her underwater vision. Colourful fish flitted past, but she knew better than to try and spear them. Firstly they would simply have been too elusive, but more importantly those bright colours inevitably meant they would be at least unpleasant tasting, and possibly even poisonous. She did spy something though; a large shell that kind of looked like an ancient cavalier's helmet.

In excitement she picked it up in both hands and surfaced. The shell looked like a slightly mossy, squished softball from the outside, but inside the abalone had a shiny mother of pearl lining and a big chunk of rubbery meat.

This would make an excellent meal. As she contemplated the array of different ways she would be able to cook it, she became aware of a weird whining noise in her ear. Tapping her head to one side, she cleared all the water out of her ears, but it wasn't that. A mosquito, then? No, the air around her was bug free. Turning around to look out to sea, Sinter nearly screamed with elation.

Thundering towards her across the Blue was a speedboat. Dropping the shell instantly, she began to yell, waving her arms above her head, hollering for all she was worth. She didn't care any more if it was a tender from the *Moumoku Maru*, she just wanted to be found, wanted human contact so badly.

The helm of the boat was occupied by standing silhouettes, one of them with their arms also held aloft in a gesture of welcome and jubilation. As the distance narrowed, Sinter could identify the shape, one she knew so well.

It was Mistral. Her friend was not only alive, but was coming to her rescue.

23

Neither of the boys knew what to say. Standing alongside the hastily dug shallow grave, nothing seemed appropriate. There could be no headstone, no flowers; and no eulogy seemed to fit. As tragic as the situation was, somehow it was an inevitable, perhaps even fitting, conclusion to Wolf's short and violent life.

"He knew this was how it would end," Peregrine said simply. "At least it was on his own terms, not being taken out quietly and pumped full of drugs like a dog being put down."

"I guess in a weird way he's finally free," Saker added. "And he went down fighting."

Peregrine nodded his assent. "Much as I'd like to hang here and chew the fat with the deceased, we've wasted enough time. We need to get out of here. Those drones could be back any time."

Then he turned and started off towards the setting sun,

and the nearest town. Saker, however, took an extra minute, dropping to one knee alongside the freshly turned over soil.

"I never thought I'd say this," he confided to the earth beneath him, "but I'm sorry. We're just the same, you and I. You were my brother, even if we did end up hating each other. You were manipulated just like me. You were just doing all you could to survive. I don't blame you, or any of the others. It's him I blame."

Thoughts of the Prophet coursed through his mind, their cruel leader who had been the orchestrator of all of their agony.

"I promise you this, Wolf," he said. "I promise I'll make him pay."

And with that he took the wooden bullet from his pocket, and placed it on the grave.

Standing, he broke into a jog and headed off to catch up with his new ally.

In the nearest village, over an apple juice in the local store, the two usually taciturn boys put their heads together, and tried to come up with a plan.

"First thing is to get as far away from here as possible, hopefully across the border," Peregrine insisted. "The Clan have our last position, and know we are together. They will descend on this place with everything they have."

"We should get clean out of the country," Saker agreed. "Do you have credentials?"

"I do," Peregrine replied, "but not here. I have a stash to the north. What about you?"

"Mine's in completely the opposite direction," Saker said. "We should split up."

"Well let's recce where Wolf suggested," Peregrine said.

"Majestic?" Saker asked. "It will take me a while to get there."

"That gives us a chance to throw them off the scent; walk with our shoes on backwards."

Saker knew exactly what he meant. Poachers will sometimes tie another pair of shoes onto the underside of their own, orientated back to front. Rangers tracking them will think their footprints are leading in the opposite direction. It's classic misdirection.

"We'll take one phone each," Saker added. "If I get caught, then contact my friend Minh in Vietnam. He'll know what to do."

The boys didn't shake hands. Somehow that didn't seem sufficient. The import of what they were about to do hung over them like a curse; words unspoken, fear not yet confronted.

Falcons are generally solitary, hunting alone, fearing any challenge on their own territory and space. Saker falcons are one of the only species that will hunt together, using their own kind as allies. One bird will fly low, hidden by bushes or a fence line, while the other hammers into a flock of pigeons, startling them into flight. Only when the scattered prey take to the air will the second bird appear, scything in to make an instant and brutal kill. It's always an uneasy alliance, but one which can make the birds of prey more effective.

With Sinter, Saker had always felt ill at ease. Her caring human side conflicted with his own combative, ferocious instinct. He always wanted to tackle a problem head on, while she would rather let caution, reason and thoughtfulness drive her plans. But Peregrine was an ally who tackled problems in the same way he did. A peregrine is the fastest creature ever to have lived. Classically they will soar up high, putting the sun behind them so they dazzle their avian prey. At the crucial moment they will drop from the heavens like a bullet, in a dive known as a stoop. They hit their prey at close to two hundred miles an hour, an irresistible and unstoppable force.

Operating at such speeds there is no time for thought. Instinct is everything. And Saker's instinct told him that Peregrine could be trusted; he didn't have the guile to be deceptive. Now that his course was set, he would stoop towards it with singularity of purpose. Either his prey would perish, or he would hammer into the ground with fatal force.

But now, out of nowhere, Saker's thoughts turned to Sinter. His mind had been so full of simply staying alive that she hadn't intruded into his consciousness in days. Now that she came back to the recesses of his thoughts, there was a pang he didn't recognise, a tugging in his chest. He saw her like a portrait in slow motion. Amber eyes like the tigress she so resembled, dark hair moving about her shoulders like smoke. In the past he had felt an inexplicable urge to take care of her, to put his body in front of Sinter and protect her. How had he let her slip so far? He didn't even know where she was!

Rummaging into his back pocket, he produced a battered old phone, the kind that emerges from down the side of a sofa, believed lost for years. Pressing the on button, he was rewarded with an old-fashioned screen. Scrolling down the list of contacts, he came to a name. It said "Taxi", but that was just an innocuous name that snoopers would never look at. It was actually the number of the phone he'd left in Sinter's possession.

Suddenly he had an overwhelming need to speak to her, to find out if she was all right, to tell her all of his plans. Normally he would have fought the urge, or another thought would have taken him before he could do anything. But this time the strongest drive was to find her.

He pressed call. The phone went straight to voicemail. He thought for a second about leaving a message. About confessing that he was thinking about her, telling her how much she meant to him, how he was missing her. He wanted to apologise for the life he had condemned her to, and had a sudden urge to save her from all the danger he'd unwittingly exposed her to. But all that was way too much to say in a voicemail. As the tone sounded, he hung up. Another problem; to be dealt with another time.

*

Two days later, and both boys were already in different countries, covering their tracks as they went. Peregrine crossed by night over the land border into Slovakia, while Saker caught a local bus in completely the opposite direction. With his dark eyes and hair, Saker still blended in with the locals. With his hoody always raised, and an insolent, angry look on his face, he judged that no one would try and talk to him, therefore never realising he didn't speak the language.

In Belgium, he bought a cheap laptop, so he could finally get in touch with Minh. Minh was one of the most unusual but valuable contacts they'd made in their time as fugitives in Vietnam – a computer genius with a talent for the shady side of hacking. Though Minh was on the other side of the world, he was only an internet connection away.

Saker had found a little-used storeroom in a run-down area of town to sleep the night and, sitting on the sacks of rice that were to be his bed, he switched the laptop on, and connected. Minh had set up a fake website that claimed to sell computer parts. By logging on to it and applying to buy one obscure piece of kit, he was signalling to Minh that he wanted to be contacted. This meant that Saker didn't have to worry about bypassing all the spyware and hackers who would inevitably be watching over Minh and his online presence.

It was two hours later that an internet call came through. The boys hadn't spoken for a year, and much had happened in the interim. However, Minh had never been one for pleasantries. His face flashed up on the screen, looking, as always, slightly irritated.

"What is it?" he said, not even asking Saker what country he was in, or if he was in danger.

Saker sighed inwardly. Minh had never been much good at being friends with anyone. However, his talents were undeniable. Without them, Saker would surely have been killed ten times over. And here, in this terrifying new world where the Clan was discovering modern methods of hunting, Minh would be even more important than ever before.

"Are we on a secure line?" Saker asked.

"Secure? I have a more secure system than the CIA," Minh answered. Saker almost fancied he sounded slightly offended. That was a first.

"Good. Cos I need your help."

Saker picked up the smartphone, and held it in front of the laptop's camera. "The Clan are now carrying smartphones, and co-ordinating their actions using them. Their missions are sent out by the Prophet through these, using 3D holograms. I want to hack them."

Minh looked back over the internet hook up, and nibbled his lip with what looked uncomfortably like concern.

"I presume there are pretty intense security protocols to get into that phone?" he queried.

"Yup," Saker responded. "Fingerprint scan; but I have that one covered."

With that, he opened a small box from his pocket, and peeled off what looked rather like a disgusting slice of dead skin.

"Smart!" Minh said, sounding appreciative.

Saker smiled. He had been rather proud of this one. Just before they had buried Wolf, Saker had applied successive layers of superglue to Wolf's thumb. When they built up enough, he had peeled them off as one. The underside revealed a perfect thumbprint in relief.

"You need to make a reverse print of that though," Minh advised. "Or the print will be backwards."

Saker closed his eyes and groaned. He hadn't thought of that.

"I'll get some polymorph," he replied gratefully. Polymorph was melted plastic that could be formed into any shape. Pressed into the print like a mould, it should give the thumbprint exactly as it had appeared on Wolf's thumb. It was one of the few items of kit with so many applications that he carried some around with him everywhere.

"It also has a retinal scan," Saker added, "but hopefully we've got that covered too."

He explained that he had shone a flashlight into Wolf's eyes, and taken a photo looking in through the lens. Minh could use that photo to generate a complex model of the back of Wolf's eyeball. It was cutting edge hacking, and should give them access to the phone.

"The only thing is," Saker ventured, "we can't turn the

phone on. The Clan have it tracked, and the second it's on, it'll broadcast where I am."

"That's easy," scoffed Minh. "You just need to obscure the signal. Put it in a metal box while you turn it on, then switch off the broadcast function once you're into it."

Hmmm . . . easier said than done.

"Wait there a second." Saker searched through the storeroom for something that might work. Amazingly, in the basement he found a huge old iron safe. Giggling to himself at the madness of it all, Saker positioned the laptop outside of it on a packing box, and climbed inside. Then, taking a deep breath, he pressed the on button.

The screen lit up. *Fingerprint scan required.* Holding his breath, Saker pressed the polymorph thumb onto the sensor. The screen blinked twice, and then abruptly the home screen appeared. He was in! And the safe walls were shutting off any phone signal. As quickly as possible he went straight into the options, and switched the phone into airplane mode.

"It worked!" he told Minh as he climbed out of the safe.

"So do you have any other surprises for me?" Minh asked.

"Just the one," Saker responded, revealing a metal box about the size of a cigarette package.

"A hard drive?" Minh queried.

"Yup, we found it in the Clan's laboratory. I'm sure they will have wiped it though."

Minh scoffed. "That doesn't mean anything; you can never truly wipe those things. They'll always leave a memory there somewhere. You just need to know where to look."

With the phone and hard drive plugged into the laptop, Minh took control, and went silent. Saker sat back, knowing he was in for a long wait.

Saker and Sinter were walking down a long beach, waves crashing noisily upon the shore. Pelicans skimmed the surface; the sun sparkled like fire on the water. Shoulder to shoulder, they stepped in unison, not speaking, not needing to. All was said. The water thrashed around Sinter's calves, splashing her dress. She laughed, and sprayed water at Saker, who joined in, driving his hand through the waves to drench her. But then the water turned, and Sinter's face changed, suddenly rent with concern, then horror, as the current ripped her from the shore.

She was in deep, arms held up above the swell, being tugged out to sea by the undertow. Saker called out, wading out after her, but the tow was too strong. It was carrying her further and further away from him.

"Saker!" she called, and again, "Saker, SAKER!"

He woke up, finding himself lying on the rice sacks.

"Saker!" the laptop called at him. "Saker!"

It was Minh, calling to him over the connection. Saker swung his legs down and sat up. His neck hurt from lying awkwardly.

"Sorry, Minh," he grumbled. "I fell asleep."

He looked at the clock on the laptop. 5 a.m. When Minh got to work, sleep was an unnecessary inconvenience.

"I've hacked it." Minh seemed excited, triumphant. "I generated a reverse retinal scan using the photo you sent me. Good work thinking of that, by the way."

Saker grimaced, rubbing his neck. "So what have we got?"

"Well, breaking into the phone is one thing," Minh reasoned. "But what you want me to do is next level. I need more phones, more data, more to work with."

Saker grimaced again. "I had a horrible feeling you were going to say something like that."

Over the course of the next week, Saker made his way by train and bus across the continent. So many of the places he travelled through seemed familiar to him, but he was never sure if they were real memories, or just artificial ones placed there by postcards and TV programmes.

So much from his young life was uncertain; everything before his awakening with the tiger was hazy. The long journey gave Saker hours and hours to sit and think. He thought about his past, about the family he had never known. Surely he couldn't merely have been born in a test tube? He knew enough of science to know there must have been a mother and father, even if they were merely donors. And even though they had played no part in his upbringing, those strangers were his only family. He had to find them somehow, or his curiosity would plague him for eternity.

Finally he found himself watching the scenery of northern France whizz by outside the window, and then abruptly disappear as the train ducked into the tunnel beneath the English Channel.

The next stop would be London, home to the recce point known as Majestic.

24

Alone raven sat on the back of a garden bench, cronking its deep-throated, raspy call. Behind it, the ancient stone walls of the world's most famous prison soared, near white against the grey London sky.

Raven, thought Saker, looking through a small pair of binoculars, *that'd be a good Clan animal; clever, strong, acrobatic flier* . . . and then he snickered as the bird dropped down onto the lawn right in front of a "Stay off the grass" sign, and began hopping around on both feet, looking for scraps. *Of course around here they mostly feed on tourist's sandwiches, so they're not exactly lethal.*

With that, he swung the binoculars round the Tower of London's central green. The highest levels of security of any public place in Europe; body and bag scans just to get inside; no escape once you were within; plus being public and incredibly busy, made Majestic an unbeatable recce point.

"Nothing yet," he spoke into a small plastic walkie-talkie.

They'd picked them up for a tenner each from a toyshop nearby, but they worked perfectly well and had got through the scans, which professional equipment might not have done.

"I hear you. Nothing going on here either," Peregrine responded.

"Activation was precisely thirteen hundred hours, so thirty minutes passed," Saker said. "It could happen anytime."

"Agreed. Eyes on, will confirm ASAP."

The two boys had met up at Majestic the previous morning. No hugs, high fives or grand gestures. Instead they had gone for a wander around Central London, focusing on gentlemen's outfitters, wigmakers, opticians and fancy dress shops. The result was remarkably effective. Both had added many years to their real ages. Peregrine had gone the whole hog with greying hair, wrinkles drawn on at the eyes and a furrowed forehead. A brown jacket and slightly stooped gait completed the impression.

Saker had gone for the image of a foreign tourist, clothes unusually colourful for a Londoner: bright backpack worn over both shoulders, "London' cap covering his head. At the last minute he had walked past a tour guide handing out coloured tabards, which would help the guide identify his particular tour group. This went over the top of his clothes, so he seemed to be part of the guided party. Slightly tinted sunglasses and a small moustache obscured a good deal of his face.

"Our mothers wouldn't recognise us," Saker japed, ". . . if we knew who our mothers were."

"Or our father," Peregrine commented.

"Father?" Saker asked. "Singular? Are you suggesting we're brothers?"

Peregrine turned away at that, suddenly grim. "It's nothing. Slip of the tongue."

The plan was a simple one, but needed to be carried out with absolute precision. To be caught by the authorities within the walls of the Tower would bring things to a messy end. Likewise if they were identified by the Clan whilst they were inside, they'd be in trouble. Eventually the day would come to an end, the Tower would close and they'd be thrown out onto the streets, and the Clan would surely be waiting. So it was high risk, but if it worked, the payoff could be huge.

Just before one o'clock in the afternoon, Peregrine and Saker had split up within the Tower, with Peregrine hanging around at the entrance and Saker waiting just inside. Then, as the clock struck one, they opened up the walkie-talkies for the first time.

"This is a comms check," Saker started. "Can you hear me out there?"

"Affirmative. These things aren't bad for kids' toys."

"OK, well here goes nothing. Powering up." Taking a

deep breath, Saker pressed the on button on the Clan phone, and watched the screen flicker into life. "Good luck brother."

He then placed the phone in his pocket and went back to pretending to study ravens, and the Yeomen of the Guard, who were wandering past in their extravagant uniforms. He took care to stand right in the centre of the plaza, so his phone signal wouldn't be blocked by the metre-thick stone walls, knowing his position was being transmitted up to a satellite and on to the Clan, wherever they might be.

It was forty-five minutes before the radio crackled into life, giving Saker a leap of anticipation.

"OK, we have action," Peregrine spoke into the walkie-talkie. "Two boys, clearly Clan, scoping things out and headed towards the entrance."

"Do you recognise either of them?" Saker asked.

"No, pretty much your classic Clan robots. One is wearing a long black overcoat. He looks like a psycho Paddington Bear." Saker giggled at that description.

"The other," Peregrine continued, "has on a black bomber jacket with a grey hoody over the top."

"Any distinguishing features?" Saker asked.

Peregrine paused, clearly chancing a longer look at the two, as they pretended to be examining ice-cream vans and signposts. "Yes," he answered eventually, "Paddington has a nasty scar down the left side of his face. And one eye is completely white. Looks like a chemical burn."

Saker pricked up his ears. "Oil," he said. "It wasn't chemicals, it was boiling oil."

He then closed his eyes and cursed under his breath. He knew who it was. It was Margay. One of the first Clan boys who had pursued him and Sinter as they made their escape in northern India. As they fled through a busy market, Sinter had kicked a pan of boiling oil all over him, scorching his face. It had probably been the first moment that Saker realised quite how capable his female counterpart was.

There was a pang in his chest. What was that? Was it a twinge of concern? Was he missing her? Or was it just a lunge of panic, realising that everything was going to be that much harder now that one of the boys knew him well?

"They're splitting up," Peregrine continued. "Paddington is hanging behind and bringing up the rear, bomber jacket is heading in."

"So Paddington's our mark," Saker answered. "I'm heading to the scanners."

Outside the Tower, Peregrine made a beeline towards Margay, weaving through the tourist hordes nonchalantly, as if he was just wandering. As he got closer, his hand slipped up the back of his own jacket, then re-emerged cupped and clearly concealing something. Clasped under his palm was the glint of steel. It was a throwing knife; the blade short, but with a wicked jagged trailing edge. The razor-sharp blade lay flat, hidden against his forearm, poised, ready.

Using the crowds as a smokescreen, he approached, like a stalking leopard crawling towards a drinking gazelle. When Margay was just metres ahead, Peregrine clenched his fingers around the knife handle and brought it into an underhand stabbing position. Drawing his arm back, he approached from Margay's bad eye side, and bumped bodily into him as if by accident, bringing the knife rapidly forward.

"Eh, watch where you're going, señor!" Peregrine snarled in a Spanish accent.

Margay looked around him in confusion, but the cause of the collision was already gone.

When he was a safe distance away, Peregrine dared to turn back. The Clan boy in the bomber jacket had already gone into the Tower. Margay had not been put off his course, and had continued to the scanners. Peregrine turned now, took off his brown jacket and turned it inside out to reveal the blue interior, putting it back on again as he walked. Now he doubled back, and dropped into the queue behind Margay.

Margay had no bag to put through the scanning machine, but took a smartphone from his pocket and placed it on the belt. The security guard beckoned him forward, and Margay stepped through the metal detecting archway. It beeped and lights flashed red. Margay looked down at the lights in utter confusion; he knew he didn't have anything on him that would set the alarms off. The burly policeman beckoned him over and asked him to spread his arms wide, then ran a hand scanner over him from the head down. He only got as far as the pockets of the Paddington coat before the thing started to beep madly.

The policeman reached forward into the pocket and drew out the throwing blade with the jagged edge that Peregrine had surreptitiously dropped into his pocket in their engineered collision. Now, as a bewildered Margay struggled to explain himself to two very stern-looking policemen, Peregrine walked through the metal detector himself, nonchalantly picked up Margay's phone from the conveyor belt, and kept walking.

Once away from the growing fray around Margay's arrest, he took the phone out of his pocket, and turned it face up. He then took a slice of tape from his pocket and placed it over the fingerprint sensor before peeling it away, taking a perfect Margay thumbprint with it.

Saker now stood right in the middle of the green at the centre of the Tower. He had no idea quite how accurate the GPS locator would be, and it was pretty crowded. And then he saw him. Black bomber jacket and grey hoody, just as Peregrine had said. He knew him instantly. It was Mako, named after the fastest shark on the planet.

Saker headed straight for him, maintaining his round-shouldered gait, head turned down to the ground. When the two were almost face to face, Saker straightened, took off his glasses and moustache and unveiled himself. Mako's eyes almost popped out of their sockets. He instantly raised his cuff to his mouth, clearly speaking into a hidden microphone.

"It's over, Saker," Mako said. "You're coming with us now."

"I don't think so," Saker responded.

"You're outnumbered, and pretty soon the Prophet will have an army outside, ready to bring you in." Mako spoke as if he was reading from a script. Robotically.

"Well, that's all a matter of perception," Peregrine said from behind him, with one hefty hand falling on Mako's shoulder. "Two to one . . . seems like *you're* outnumbered to me."

"But my backup—" Mako began.

"Is presently being loaded into a police wagon," finished Saker.

Mako's head flickered around him, suddenly cowed, well aware that he was on the back foot. "What do you want from me?"

"That's easy. We just want your phone," Saker said.

"My phone?" Mako was even more confused now.

"This phone, to be precise." Peregrine was brandishing it in his hand – he had already expertly picked his pocket.

"But . . . you don't think you'll get away with this, do you? We'll pick you up within the hour!"

Saker tilted his head to one side and pursed his lips. "I'm willing to take that chance. In the meantime, swap you."

With that, he passed Mako a present, neatly wrapped, and about the size of a box of tissues.

"Open it," Peregrine advised. "I promise it's not a bomb."

Mako looked at the box as if it was about to explode. He pulled the ribbon and it fell off, then he lifted the lid. Inside was a wicked-looking but unusual hunting knife. With a mixture of fascination and befuddlement he took it out of the wrapping and held it in his hands.

How about that? he thought. *It's made of ceramic.* And then the penny dropped. *Ceramic, so it would slip through the metal detectors unnoticed.* When he looked up again, the two boys were gone. But in their place, two policemen were running towards him.

"That's him!" one of them shouted.

Mako dropped the knife and ran, but there was nowhere to go. He was still shouting his innocence when Peregrine and Saker bound different Underground trains, already wearing different disguises and heading to opposite ends of the capital, both fingering the precious treasures in their pockets. Stage one of the grand plan was complete.

25

Sinter had never been hugged like that in her memory. Perhaps her mother had held her this way before she passed away, but that was so long ago she couldn't recall. All she knew was that Mistral's embrace seemed to last a lifetime, and took all the pain away.

"I thought you were dead," Mistral finally said.

"I thought *you* were dead!" Sinter replied with a stifled laugh in her voice. She realised that she was crying, that the salty tears were like acid in the sunburn cracks in her cheeks and lips. But she didn't care.

"How did you make it?" Sinter asked. "There was nobody at the surface when the *Galeocerdo* was capsized."

"There was an airspace underneath the boat," Mistral explained. "I popped up into that, and waited. I thought when the *Maru* came back they were going to bulldoze over the top of us and I'd be history, but then they just seemed to slow right down."

"They stopped to pick me up," Sinter said, "but then, just an hour later, they made me walk the plank!"

"Figures," Mistral spat. "There is nothing those vile longliners won't do. And ever since, you've been stranded on a desert island!"

"Yup, I'm such a cliché," laughed Sinter. "I thought that only happened in the movies!"

"It was a whole day floating there under the motorboat before the *Shark Saviour* found me." Mistral was suddenly quiet, sombre.

"And the captain? And Manta? And the others?" Sinter's concern became horror. She'd been so busy thinking about Mistral, she hadn't thought of the others. Mistral's eyes were cast down to the deck. She shook her head.

Now the tears flowed freely down Sinter's cheeks, but they were tears of guilt and anguish rather than joy. Guilt that she had been so busy thinking about herself that she hadn't thought about the others. Pain because they were gone and she'd never seen them again. Granted she'd never been friends with Manta and they had nothing in common, but the girl was only young, and had wanted to change the world. She would never get to fall in love, to have children, to see the world like she had wanted.

And the captain. He had been a good man. Someone who had seen so much, and done so much to make the world a better place. The thought that he was gone for ever was the greatest heartache she could ever remember.

Back on the *Shark Saviour*, Sinter was welcomed like a returning heroine, with kisses and hugs and cheers, but there was a sense that things were far from right. The whole crew was in mourning for the passing of their leader. Several of them had decided to end their time on board, having realised now that the stakes were simply too high. There was a huge worry that once the investors knew that the ship had no captain, they would pull out and leave the *Shark Saviour* without funding.

These were uncertain and harrowing times, and it seemed the whole team might be about to collapse. That evening, Sinter and Mistral stood watching the stars, up on the deck of the boat.

"What do you know about stars?" Mistral asked.

"OK, that's a pretty big question," Sinter answered. "I know they're a really long way away."

"Well, yes and no." Mistral smiled. "The stars themselves may be light years gone, some of them could have died thousands of years ago and we're just seeing their extinct light . . ." Sinter waited for her to continue. "But their stories, their stories are all human. From ancient Roman and Greek myths."

"So tell me some."

"Well, that's Ganymede," Mistral said, pointing to a group of stars as if they were a join-the-dots picture, "abducted from a simple and happy life by a cruel god, and made to do his bidding."

Sinter tried to make out the picture behind the sparkling

dots that were punctuating the blackness above her head. That sounded familiar. Well, apart from Saker being a god, of course.

"And that's Andromeda," said Mistral, pointing to another part of the sky, and tracing the shape of a girl in the firmament. "And do you see that white blur by her right hip?"

"It just looks like a smear – like a smudge," answered Sinter.

"That smudge is billions of stars, a whole galaxy – the furthest astronomical object visible to the naked eye."

"So what's her story?"

"Andromeda was a real heroine," Mistral started. "Humble, beautiful, kind . . . but her weak father, the king, sacrificed her to Poseidon the ocean god, then married her off to a stranger, rather than risk his own skin."

Sinter turned and looked at Mistral. The darkness was cut by a little weak yellow light spilling from the cabin door. Not enough to read what was going on behind Mistral's dark eyes. They'd never talked about Sinter's past before, about how her father had betrayed her and attempted to sell her in an arranged marriage. How much did Mistral know?

Sinter said, with a hint of sarcasm, "As if a father would ever do that to his daughter!"

"Quite," answered Mistral, fixing Sinter's gaze as if looking into her soul.

Sinter's mind raced. Mistral was very perceptive, and

didn't really need to know any specifics. After all, Sinter was a young high-born Indian girl on the run, with an unknown source of wealth and no connection to her family or roots. Anybody with a bit of nous could work out that she was on the run from an arranged marriage.

"It's a bit of a stretch to join the dots and see all that," Sinter said, tearing her eyes away.

"Andromeda is always portrayed chained by the wrists to rocks as the sea lashes at her feet, ready to be devoured by a sea monster. It's as if she's condemned to a million lifetimes of torment, that she can never truly escape and be free."

Sinter's response was so quiet Mistral could barely hear her words; "How do you know so much about me?"

"I don't. These stories are two thousand years old. And people will be looking up at the stars in two thousand years' time and seeing their own lives reflected back at them then too. You're not alone, Sinter. Your life may be difficult, it may seem cruel and as if you are the first person ever to go through all this. But no one in human history has gone through life without hard times, and without pain. I understand that you feel you have to tackle the whole world without anyone's help. But it doesn't have to be that way."

"You don't understand; it's different for me."

"I don't have to understand everything. Or anything, really. All I have to do is be here, and give you what I can."

The silence that followed was laden with words unspoken, with weeks, months and years of fear and mistrust. Sinter would have given anything for another of those all-enveloping hugs. Tears started to run down her face. Normally she would have been embarrassed and furiously scrubbed them away as a sign of weakness. Now she just let them flow.

"I've been looking over my shoulder so long," she whispered, "I don't know how to look forward any more."

"It ends well for Andromeda. She *is* set free, she finds true love, and Athena places her image up there in the sky to honour her."

"Well, that's all right for her – she's just a figment of some dead guy's imagination."

Mistral laughed out loud. "Fair enough. I'll quit with the star nonsense."

"No, don't," Sinter said. Somehow it was easier to talk about things that mattered through the empty void of space. "What's that one up there?"

"That's my constellation!" Mistral said. "The fish."

"Pisces?" Sinter felt as if she should know the story, and was loathe to ask.

"Yes. In Greek mythology they represent two characters – Aphrodite and Eros, sometimes known as Cupid and Venus. They were in danger of being torn apart, so they leapt into a stream together and transformed into two fishes, then they tied themselves together at the tail so they would never be apart."

"I've always thought that if you were Clan, you'd be a fish," Sinter said. "Maybe a silky shark?"

Mistral looked at her quizzically. "As long as I'm not a haddock."

"Look!" Sinter blurted. "A shooting star!"

"That's not a shooting star," said Mistral. "Watch the way it continues on a perfect parabola trajectory. It's a satellite, probably flying twenty thousand miles up, maybe for television or something."

A satellite. Something tugged at the back of Sinter's brain. Why did satellites have such a strong relevance to what they were talking about? She thought back to Russia, to the satellite images they'd sent of illegal oil drilling in the Arctic refuge. To Minh in Vietnam . . .

"I can get us the money we need," she blurted.

Mistral looked at her. "What d'you mean? We're talking proper cash here. It costs hundreds of thousands to keep this boat and crew going every year. I mean, it's not pocket money, you know."

Sinter ignored the slightly patronising air of her friend. "I know that. But I can get proper money. You just get me to a port where I can get online, and I promise I'll have you all the money you need by the following morning."

Mistral looked Sinter straight in the eye. "I should just laugh at that. I mean, if you were anyone else I'd think you were nuts." Then, taking her by the hand, she continued, "But nothing you say surprises me any more. And everything you say you can do, you do."

Sinter squeezed Mistral's hand, and looked out to the black waves tossing in front of them. "I've been running for a long time now, and I'm sick of it. I've found what I need here, what I want to do and who I want to be with. It's time to start paying it back."

The Maori girl's dark eyes were now alight with possibility, plans, potential. She could barely contain herself. "I'll gather the crew," she said.

An hour later and the entire crew of the *Shark Saviour* were standing up on the decks, under the Southern Cross and Jupiter – shining solidly with its many moons barely perceptible to the naked eye. The Milky Way stretched across the sky as if a giant star god had smudged his work while painting the night sky. They stood shoulder to shoulder while Mistral spoke.

"We all have a choice right now. We're all here for a reason. Maybe you're running away from something, maybe you want to make a difference." Then she chanced a look at Sinter. "Maybe both. But I'm telling you now, none of that matters. If you need a family, look around you. If you need a cause, look at what we can achieve together."

Sinter smiled; her friend had a way with words, and with people.

"Our friends have paid the ultimate price, and I understand that some of you will think that is too much to risk. Tomorrow we pull into port in Halmahera. None of us will think badly of you if you choose to leave us there. To those that stay, I promise this. We will make a difference.

Every one of you will be able to look back on your time on the *Shark Saviour* and know that you did something to save our seas. That you stood up and were counted. That you let the evil scum like those murderers on the *Moumoku Maru* know that what they're doing is wrong. That their crimes will be punished, and that our friends – our family – did not die for nothing."

"What about money?" called out one of the crew. "All the backers have gone. How're we going to pay for food and fuel?"

"Actually," Mistral responded, "we have money." Then, looking at Sinter again, who returned her smile, she continued. "In fact, more money than we've ever had. We may even be able to stretch to tofu and tempe, on top of the two-week-old lettuces."

There were general murmurs among the crew, and they seemed to be positive.

"If you'll have me, I'll take over the captaincy," Mistral added. "If not, we can have some kind of election." At this there were general reactions that showed this would not be necessary.

"OK then," she assented. "Let's go back out there as a team, and let's make the evil men who want to empty our seas . . . let's make them pay."

The following morning, the *Shark Saviour* rolled into port in Halmahera in the Spice Islands. It's a decent-sized city with a telephone antenna on the headland just outside, and as the ship neared shore everyone's mobile phones got signal for the first time in a fortnight. Suddenly the boat decks rang to the sound of text messages arriving, and crewmembers scuttled off to find private places to call family, who probably didn't know if they were alive or dead.

Sinter knew her family would not be calling. They had no idea where she was or how to contact her and, though it saddened her, she no longer felt that she had no one. Now she had a new family, and she was right here on the boat. Sinter went below decks to her bunk, in amongst the ventilation pipes and with the constant clanging of the propellers making the walls vibrate, and opened her small locker. She didn't own much, but would need to pack up pretty much all of it to go ashore for a few days.

There, sitting in the bottom of the locker, was a phone. An impossibly old-fashioned mobile phone with no smart touch screen, but a battery life that lasted for ever. And the screen was illuminated, with a single icon on it. The icon of a letter.

Sinter's brow furrowed. There was only one person in the world who still had this phone number. She picked it up, and opened the message.

I know how to bring down the Clan, it read. *I have information. We need to meet. Recce point Babylon.*

And that was it. Sinter threw the phone down on her bunk with disgust and leaned, eyes closed, with her head against the bulkhead wall. Why? Why was he always doing this to her? This was his fight, not hers. She'd found a life for herself, the chance of making a positive future where she didn't have to run any more. And yet again, he'd come stampeding in bringing chaos and danger. If he'd been there, she'd have slapped him in his stupid face.

Recce point Babylon? That was on the other side of the world! Who barks orders demanding someone drop everything and fly three thousand miles? Throwing her head back, she let loose with a roar of rage.

"I have a problem," Sinter told Mistral and then, seeing the look of concern on her face, went on, "Don't worry, it's not the money. That will be with you all tomorrow. It's just a loose end I need to tie off. I'll be gone a fortnight, maybe a month."

"Don't worry," said Mistral. "This boat isn't going anywhere without you."

"No," said Sinter wearily. "I need you to carry on. Where I'm going, there could be . . . complications." She sighed. With Saker there were always complications. "But I'll find you, and I'll be back as soon as I've finished with this. For good."

What Sinter didn't say was, "There's a chance I might never come back. There always is."

The boat docked in the noisy harbour, surrounded by bulbous wooden Makassar schooners, crossing the archipelago laden with cloves, cardamom and sandalwood.

Sinuous men with sweat-drenched torsos ferried the cargo up and down planked gangways into and out of town. The heady scents filled the air and made Sinter light-headed. Baby-blue fishing boats loaded crates of dried baitfish and squid, and haggled for fuel and fruit. Thundering trucks and motorised tuktuks battled to drown out the shouting of men as they argued, along with the crowing of cockerels and the bleating of harbour-side goats. The bustle, noise and life closed in on Sinter like a dark cloak after months at sea with only the wind and seagulls as her soundtrack.

Mistral took Sinter in another embrace, one that shut the rest of the world out and made everything right. Taking her face in her hands, she kissed her on the cheek.

"Always remember, Sinter," she said, "we are here for you, and we are your family now. We don't care about your past – just about you."

A chain of sweating porters pushed past them carrying bundles of provisions, breaking the moment somewhat.

"It's a little cheesy, but my mum always used to say to me, 'The past is history, the future is a mystery; but now is a gift – that's why it's called the present'."

Sinter giggled. It *was* a little cheesy.

"But you get done what you've got to get done," Mistral soothed, "and then you come back to us. And then you stop running."

Sinter smiled. And then she had a thought. Reaching over her neck, she removed the chain and the locket containing her mother's photo. Her most treasured possession, and the only memorial she had of her past life. She placed it over Mistral's dark hair, and the locket settled at her throat.

"I want you to take care of this for me, Mistral," she said. "It's the only picture I have of my mother, the only thing I have that really means anything to me. Well . . ." she began to correct herself, but Mistral stopped her.

"I'll take good care of it. And I'll be giving it back to you in just a few weeks. Godspeed, little Tigress."

And with that, she kissed her on the cheek, and walked back on board, turning her back so Sinter wouldn't see the tears building in her eyes.

Sinter walked down the boardwalk to port, a small red child's rucksack on her back, containing everything she owned. The second she hit solid land, her legs turned to jelly – the whole world was going up and down. She started to feel seasick . . . well, landsick!

Her first call was to an internet café to contact Minh and organise the money. Her second was to buy a plane ticket. Actually, a series of plane tickets. To get to the recce with Saker, she would have to span the globe on a series of long-haul flights that would take her to Jakarta, Singapore, Bahrain in the Middle East and finally to the desert Kingdom of Jordan.

While her fellow plane passengers slept, or watched movies, Sinter spent her time staring out of the windows and thinking. She thought of all the lives she'd managed to

216

build for herself since leaving India. She had found comfort and purpose in the slums of Vietnam, working to help the sick. She smiled at the memory of her Irish friend Roisin – flame-haired, fiery-tempered, accepting of Sinter with all her flaws and hidden history. Roisin could have been family, but Saker and the Clan came stampeding in and ruined it all. She couldn't even email Roisin any more, in case it put everyone in danger.

She thought of her friends in the Arctic Yamal. The reindeer herding family who had saved her life, nursed her back to health, and showed her a way of life of brutal, simple beauty. Saker had gate-crashed that party as well, and she could never go back. Everywhere he went, he brought pain and anarchy. And despite her ties to him, they were barely friends. When had he ever asked how she felt about something? When had he ever cared about her feelings like Mistral did, cared about her ambitions like Roisin, or even protected her wellbeing like the herdsmen had?

All Saker thought about was himself, and his own obsession. Granted, he was capable; physically and mentally exceptional. If he could be shown the right way, he had phenomenal potential and genuinely could change the world. But in his soul he was all darkness, self-obsession, introspection. It was like trying to talk sense to a honey badger that had its mind set on a beehive or chasing off a pride of lions.

And Sinter was through with trying. In the past she had

tussled with her feelings for him. There was no doubt the two of them made a handsome couple, and having someone strong by her side who could protect her . . . it seemed she'd always been told that was what she should want. But in reality, the only reason she needed any protection was because of the trouble Saker had brought her! For years now, when she thought of Saker, there was a tangle in her guts that she couldn't explain; was it the connection you might feel for a brother? Was it love? She didn't feel that tangle any more. Where before she had felt confused, now she felt nothing. For the first time, when she thought of Saker there was no hint of doubt.

Looking out of the plane window she could see the gleaming blue of the Mediterranean, shimmering gold in the sunlight below her. Then, abruptly, they hit the shores of Israel, and she saw the sprawling, concrete city of Tel Aviv. Then, just as abruptly, they were above miles and miles of dust and rock, a wilderness of wanderings as parched as a mouthful of dry sand. Half an hour later, the plane was in a holding circle, descending to God only knew what.

She didn't need to wait at the carousel to collect her luggage. Everything she owned fit into the small backpack she had carried onto the plane. As she walked through customs, she could feel hostile, prying eyes falling on her. A young girl alone was even more unusual in much of the Arabic world than elsewhere. As always, she tried not to openly sigh with relief when her credentials checked out, the customs official stamped her passport and she was swept along with the other passengers, out into a new, unfamiliar world.

But it didn't stay unfamiliar for long. There, at the end of the barriers where families waited for their loved ones, was a figure she knew too well. He didn't have a placard saying "Welcome!" He wasn't bearing a bouquet of roses or lilies, and his face was partially covered by dark glasses and a peaked cap. But she would have known him anywhere.

26

The straw stirred round and round in the long glass, like a spindly cement mixer toying with froth and liquid yellow concrete. Sinter had been messing with the banana milkshake for what seemed like an infinity. They'd taken a window-side table in a local café, and ordered a drink each, neither of which had been touched. Conversation had been strained at best, silent at worst. She'd known it was going to be bad, but this was ridiculous.

"So are you planning on telling me why you've summoned me halfway round the world?" she finally demanded, at the same time mentally cross with herself for sounding so churlish.

"Summoned? I – I . . ." Saker was unsure; he hadn't expected this.

"Saker," she began, again thinking that she was starting to sound like a headmistress about to give someone a good telling off. "I have a life. Thousands of miles away. If you were so desperate to talk to me, then why didn't you just call? Or send an email like any normal person would?"

"But . . . but . . ." he stammered.

Sinter smirked to herself, she couldn't help thinking her old schoolmistress would have said "Goats butt, sheep butt; people talk in proper sentences."

"So what is it that's so important?" she asked.

Saker took a deep breath, and launched in.

"I found them – the old laboratories and Clan files – and I've hacked their mainframe; well, Minh has, obviously, I don't know about any of that."

It was pouring out of him now, like a young child telling about what had happened on a great day at the zoo. "And Wolf's dead, and there's another who's joined me, Peregrine, and we have a plan to bring the Clan down once and for all – the Prophet's going to be a problem of course, and the hacking is really tricky even for Minh, but it's happening; it's all finally coming together."

Sinter looked at him. "So what?" she said simply.

"So what?" That stopped Saker dead in his tracks. "What do you mean, so what? It's happening, our plan is working, we can do this, and then stop running for ever."

Sinter looked out of the window. This was not going to be easy. She softened her tone. "It's not *our* plan, Saker," she said. "It's your plan. And I stopped running ages ago. Around about when I last saw you, actually."

That was an understatement. Pretty much the last time they had seen each other, Sinter had been frozen, poisoned, buried in ice, chased across the Siberian snows by machine-gun wielding henchmen.

He looked at her blankly. This wasn't how he had seen this going at all. "But the Clan will hunt us down, they'll never let us rest."

"I don't think that's true, Saker. I think the only reason they'll come after me is to get to you. Without you in my life, nobody is going to hunt me down. Why would they?"

"So you're going to throw me to the dogs?" Saker said in disgust. "Just desert me?"

"I'm not the one who's done all the deserting, Saker," she replied. "I've tried everything to get through to you, to try and save you. But you don't care, you've never cared about anyone other than yourself and your selfish schemes. You thunder into everything, trying to be a spy, trying to tear the world down. Sometimes things just need building back up."

"But that's why you're here," he pleaded. "We're supposed to be doing this together. I think I may have found out who I am! Sinter, Minh may have found who my real parents are." This was his trump card. Surely she would melt at this.

"Please, Sinter, you're all I have."

"You've never needed anyone before, Saker," she said. "And I've had it with being around someone who brings me nothing but trouble, then ups and leaves whenever he feels like it. You're my bad luck charm, Saker, and I don't need any more of those in my life."

"But the world is falling apart!" Saker said. "It's full of evil people smashing things up so they can make money! They only understand one language: violence, and that's what I bring."

"I don't agree," Sinter replied. "I see so much beauty, so much worth saving. When I look at the world I see people who can make a difference, and ways we can make the world a better place. Violence is for the violent, Saker. An eye for an eye will only make the world blind."

"What idiot said that?" he scoffed.

"That would be Mahatma Ghandi," she said quietly.

"It's pretty easy for you to be down on violence, but you're perfectly happy to have me go into battle for you. You're just not willing to fight your own battles!"

"I don't want you going into battle, Saker, not for me, not for anyone. And you don't do anything on my behalf." She sighed, and took his hand. "I've tried to get through to you a million times, tried to show you that all this anger is shredding you inside. But it's too late now. I have another life, one without horror and heartache. And you're not in it."

He gaped at her, gulping like a goldfish. "But – you and I, Sinter, we're family. I always hoped . . . well, I thought . . ."

With that he looked down at her hand in his. She took it away and clasped her tepid milkshake.

"What did you think, Saker? Did you think we'd fall in love, get married, have psychotic babies and teach them how to walk and do the alphabet and break people's legs with kitchen appliances?"

Saker was speechless now. "Well, yes. No. I don't know. The first bit at least I . . ." He was lost for words.

"Listen, Saker, I believe there is still hope for you, but not while you're like this. You had a brutal life, but you were given a second chance. You justify cruelty to yourself, saying 'Just this one time', but then you do it again and again, till you don't know where the boundaries are any more. Pretty soon you'll look back and see that the brutality is all you have, and what's left behind is rotten. You'll have forgotten what it means to be human, and become as bad as the people you're trying to fight."

"But they've taken everything I have," he protested.

"I understand that," she replied, resigned. "They've taken everything from me too."

"They've even taken you from me," he whispered.

Saker stood, taking her hand and drawing her towards him in an embrace, but she firmly held him away.

"No," she said. "Forget revenge, Saker. Forget feuds. I'll help you just this one time. But one day you're going to have to stop fighting everyone around you."

"And when that day comes, run. Run away as far as you can, and don't look back, or it will consume you, and there'll be nothing left to save. There'll be no more second chances."

Saker was sitting in a dark kitchen in the middle of the night. "You must have known this day would come," he said evenly, to the woman across the table from him.

"I don't know what you mean! Who are you? Why are you here?" the woman stammered.

Saker looked at her long and hard. She was about forty years old, with long, dark hair, tousled around her shoulders. He felt bad about surprising her by showing up in her house in the middle of the night, but even though she was trembling, there was still a confident poise about her bearing that suggested she had once been an athlete. And she was already recovering her composure; clearly Lizzie was someone used to dealing with dramas.

"What right do you have to break into my house?" she said, sternly this time. She was already back on the front foot, and ready to deal with her young intruder.

"It's about your son," Saker said bluntly. The woman's eyes flicked upwards, instinctively protective towards her children, sound asleep in the rooms above her.

"Not that son," Saker stated. "Your first son."

The colour drained from Lizzie's face. She had a healthy tan, Saker noted – not a grubby brown stain from working in the garden, or an orange stain of fake tan that ended at the hairline. This had been gained sunning herself round the pool in the second home overseas. He looked around the smart town house, with its valuable paintings and artifacts, the very essence of a middle-class London family who were doing very well for themselves.

"I was always afraid one of you would turn up at my door," she said simply. "But it was so long ago now. I'd almost convinced myself to forget . . . Almost."

There was a silence, while Lizzie examined the boy in front of her keenly. He held her eyes with defiance for what seemed like for ever, but eventually found his eyes flicking away to the clock above the sink.

"How did you find me?" she asked.

"There were records buried on a hard drive," Saker replied, "and I have a friend who's really good at making machinery talk."

"They told me you'd never find me," she said, "but I didn't believe them."

"They?" questioned Saker. "Who are they?"

"You know full well who they are," she replied sadly.

"You are all exactly the same, even now. You're his mirror image."

"The Prophet?" Saker was on her words like a vulture falling on carrion. "You knew him?"

"I knew him," she whispered, but there was anger in her words. "But we didn't know what he stood for. Not until it was too late."

Saker cocked his head to one side. When she had spoken with hatred, the guile of decades had slipped. There was something in her voice, something that didn't fit with the tones of a successful London mother.

"You're not from here, are you?"

She shook her head. "And my name's not Lizzie, either."

"He recruited you?"

She half laughed. "Recruited? I suppose you could call it that. We were promised this." With that she gestured with her chin to take in everything: the Aga cooker, the expensive tapestries on the walls, the crystal chandelier above their heads. "Promised a better life."

"But to get it, you had to make a huge sacrifice." Saker's voice had softened. He was no longer the interrogator, he was the confidant.

"We had children. Then we were given new lives, new identities." She was crying softly now, the past had never been meant to come back and haunt her. "But we never saw the babies, never got to be their mothers. They were taken from us before we even got to hold them."

"And what about the experiments?" Saker pressed.

"With the Clan, with our totem animals. How did they splice our genes?"

Lizzie looked truly bewildered at that. "What?" she sputtered.

Saker didn't press. He could tell instantly she knew nothing about it, and wasn't faking it. Besides, she would not have to have seen any of that. It could all have taken place in a lab far away.

"So you really are my mother?"

"What I did, how you were born . . . that's not what being a mother is."

She stood and walked to the dresser, where a picture of her family stood. It was exactly what Saker would have predicted. The photo had clearly been taken on holiday, with a Mediterranean beachfront behind. The man alongside her was somewhat older, tall and well-built, with grey hair and a big, honest smile, the perfect father. The three children and Lizzie were all encompassed in a big protective embrace.

Saker felt a familiar pang. He had never known how it felt to be protected like that, to be a part of a family. Lizzie took the picture in her hands, as if it was made of gold, as if it really was her family, and everything she had to lose.

"I cannot go back to what I was," she said, staring at the faces of her children and husband, "and they can never know."

Saker was about to reassure her, to tell her that he

meant no harm and just wanted answers. But then, abruptly, violently, Lizzie smashed the portrait on the dresser edge. Saker jumped to his feet, fists raised, startled into life. He saw blood trickle down her clenched fists, and a drop form at the bottom of her hand and drip to the floor. Before he could protest, she had pulled the picture from the frame and discarded it on the floor.

From the space behind, in between the frame and the photo, was another photograph. But this one was aged, colours faded, edges dog-eared. She passed it to him, leaving a smear of blood across the faces. Five women, all in their early twenties, all clearly pregnant. They were standing or sitting, facing the camera, smiles fixed on their faces. In the centre was a tall girl, with her shoulders thrown back, her bearing and poise evident even then. Despite the photo being at least two decades old, it was, without doubt, Lizzie.

And then a shock that punched Saker right in the solar plexus. Standing to the side of the girls was a man – close-cropped hair, dark blue trousers and lighter blue Samurai-style tunic. Other than the cruel smile, it was like looking into a mirror.

Suddenly he realised he had been simply gaping for minutes and hadn't said a word.

"I knew the second I saw you at my table," Lizzie said. She was utterly in control now. Saker's mouth hung open, unwilling to believe.

"He was older than you are now but otherwise you are

his image. I can see him in you, in everything. In the way you talk, in your mannerisms, the way you move. You are your father's son."

"My father?" He gaped.

"Surely you've worked this all out for yourself?" she asked him. It was clear from the empty, disbelieving look on Saker's face that he most definitely had not.

"One woman can only have so many children," she went on. "That's just biology. But a man, he can have a thousand children if science is on his side."

Saker sat back down again, his head starting to spin. He felt as if he might throw up.

"The Prophet?" he asked, horrified that she might answer.

"Yes," she replied quietly. "He's your father. He's the father of every single one of you."

28

The phone blinked and vibrated, waking its owner. Scolopendra was a Clan boy with a reputation for ruthlessness, and a macabre tattoo running from neck to waist of the giant venomous centipede that was his namesake. Stretching from his mossy forest bed, he cricked his neck, yawned and looked at the phone. What he saw on the screen made him sit bolt upright, and burned away his lethargy instantly. He swiped his thumb across the sensor and the phone opened, then a holographic image evolved in front of him.

Fennec was walking down a crowded Boston city street, dodging the passersby. Hands thrust into duffel-coat pockets and beanie hat pulled down over his ears, he blended in completely, even as his phone started insistently bleeping for attention. When he saw who the message was from, he ducked into the open streetside doors of a pub's beer cellar, so he could watch it in privacy.

His namesake, the fennec fox, was no stranger to darkness, doing most of its hunting by the desert night, using its oversized ears and phenomenal hearing to locate its prey. What Fennec was about to be told was certainly the most extraordinary thing his ears had ever heard.

In the arid night of the Namib desert, the Black Eagles were gazing into the hypnotic blaze of their small fire when the message came through. They were a rarity amongst Clan boys – identical twins that had been inseparable throughout training. Not even their Clan brothers could tell the two apart, and their totem animal was perfect for that, one of the only birds of prey that routinely hunts as a pair, using strategies and working together to become more effective. Their tattoos were a mirror image of each other's, covering a shoulder with a stern silhouette.

Their phones activated at the same time, as the pair of them sat dozing around their fire in a dry cave high up on a rock outcrop. The hologram cast bizarre shadows and light shows all over the cave walls.

No matter where they were around the globe, each message began the same way. The three-dimensional head of the Prophet, appearing to them as he always did when he delivered their missions. The projections from the phones worked best where there was something in the air for the light beams to fall upon: dancing specks of dust, chalk particles, fog. In the wilds of Minnesota, Fossa saw the

Prophet's image come to life in the swirling flakes of snow tumbling from the sky, as he shivered from a cold his hi-tech clothes couldn't halt.

"This is a message to all of the loyal," it began. "We are united against a common enemy: one of our own, who has turned against us; one who could bring our world, our way of life, crashing down."

Across the world, in their many various hideouts and hideaways, Clan boys growled and snarled at the treachery. Another three-dimensional face appeared in front of them now, not speaking but rotating.

"This is Saker," the Prophet's voice hissed. "He was Clan, but is now doing all he can to tear us down."

Saker sat quietly watching his own projection: a modern day WANTED poster leaping to life from the phone Wolf had given him.

This first bit had been easy. Minh had merely hacked this section from the two phones they had taken at the Tower. The rest of it had required a lot more work.

"My first request," the Prophet continued, "is to those of you who have been wearing the special plasters I gave you."

Saker bit his lip as he watched this. Someone astute, who was looking for issues with the projection, might have noticed that the image flickered more than usual, that the Prophet was talking less than before, and perhaps even that the lip sync was not quite as perfect as it would normally be. Minh was counting on the fact that Clan boys would not be looking for technical faults, but would merely be hanging on the Prophet's every word.

"If you have one of these plasters, thank you for your trust – but you can remove it, and discard it now. You will have no more need of them."

This first instruction was an important one. Saker knew that Clan boys who were wearing the plasters would have drugs leaking slowly into their systems, keeping them compliant, keeping them easy to manipulate.

Just twenty-four hours after he himself had removed the plaster, it had been as if the fog had lifted. He had seen clearly for the first time in his whole life.

On board the *Moutoko Maru*, Knifefish and Skua both watched their projections separately from the solitude of their tiny bunks below decks. They were hidden by the lines of old socks and dripping oilskins hanging in front of their little capsules, the sound of the projections drowned out by the clanging of loose locker doors and the distant *clunk clunk* of the engines.

They barely communicated with each other, and both had their Clan tattoos covered over with make-up and clothing. Pretending not to know each other was no real effort for them. Knifefish had the totem of a fish that can kill with electricity, and Skua had a bullying, piratical seabird that catches other birds on the wing and shakes their catch from out of their bellies. Not surprisingly, the pair didn't have much in common! There was also no way they could risk the captain (who they knew as Panther) realising their true identity, and true mission. Once the message was completed they would speak to each other for the first time in months.

"At every turn, Saker has done all he can to destroy our *business*." The Prophet's intonation was inimitable, almost hissing the word he most wanted to emphasise. "First in India, he obstructed our efforts to exterminate tigers, and sell their body parts to the highest bidders."

At this the image of the Prophet blinked out and gave way to graphic images of a tigress being shot with an arrow, her cowering cubs mewing as they crawled over her body as she gasped her last breaths, then pictures of tiger corpses piled one on top of another. At this, Saker sighed with relief. The three-dimensional projections of the Prophet were the ones that had been an incredible challenge for Minh to create. The images of the dead tigers had, by comparison, been easy.

"In Southeast Asia," the voice continued, "he prevented us from aiding the largest illegal logging company, costing us and our *benefactors* millions. All this rainforest, which is now standing, home to orangutans, jungle elephants, monkeys and native tribes, all because of *him*." The montage of rainforest beauty was punctuated with shots of these animals and people in all their wonder, before cutting to shots of devastation – forests burned to the ground, animals lying as pathetic, muddy corpses amongst the smoking tree stumps.

Saker had not insisted on it being all about him out of arrogance. He just knew that Clan boys would react more dramatically to one single disloyal hate figure, rather than complicating the matter by involving Sinter and Minh.

"And then he evaded our grasp again in the snows of Siberia, preventing many hundreds of wolves being slaughtered." Again, the images cut from staggeringly intoxicating images of wolves sprinting free through the snow to shots of tatty wolf carcasses, the stacks of their pelts seeming to go on for infinity.

By now, many of the older, wiser Clan boys were starting to shift with discomfort. Something wasn't right. They had all been brought up to respect, even to worship, the wild world. And though they may have known of some small parts of a mission, they would never have been exposed to the realities of it in such a visual way. They would have believed their own personal mission to be one small out-of-character job, and never seen the bigger picture.

And now Saker and Minh delivered the *coup de grâce*. Now every Clan boy, no matter who they were, or where on the planet they were, received a projection that had been tailored and created especially for them.

Squatting over a mini camp stove in the Yukon, where he had been dispatched to assist illegal gold mining operations, Wolverine watched, first in puzzlement, and then in growing fury, at shots of his own totem animal – one of the most pound-for-pound powerful and brave beasts on earth – being caught in leg-hold traps, trying to savage off its own leg to get free, before finally being bludgeoned to death by a faceless dark figure.

Minh had made all the projections of such people as sinister and dehumanised as possible, making them seem like evil phantoms. The hope was that the Clan boys would put their own face into the image. The wolverine then had its carcass thrown alongside thousands of others, all dignity shorn as the dead-eyed body hit the back of a flatbed truck.

"He has done all he can to end our attempts to exterminate Wolverines," the Prophet's voice said over the pictures, "costing us an enormous amount of money, ensuring these animals still survive in certain wild places. He cannot be allowed to continue."

Anyone who was listening out for anomalies may have noticed the voice sounding vaguely synthesised. Surrounded by a ravaged, dry forest in Madagascar, that was Caracal's very last concern. He had just seen his own totem animal – a stunning wild cat with tufted ears – being housed in a cage not big enough to turn around in, eyes wild with fear and hatred. Caracal looked around at the forest he was helping to destroy with eyes open for the first time. He looked at his own palms, as if expecting to see them stained with blood.

In the pub basement, Fennec wiped his face with his hand, and felt it tainted with sickly sweat. What he had just seen he could never unsee, and there was a dread building in his guts, a dread he couldn't yet explain or understand. He looked at the crumpled sticking plaster in his hand, as if it were a bill that he hadn't expected to have to pay. He didn't know it yet, but when he woke the next morning, his mind would be clearing, becoming more lucid, and with the clarity would come the agony of guilt and fear. The terror that everything you know to be true is a lie.

"This much I can tell you by our new, sophisticated methods," the Prophet's voice continued. No one was paying enough attention now to notice that the voice was monotone, that syllables were being repeated exactly as they had already been before. "But the rest of your mission I must give you in person."

Fennec licked his lips with anticipation. For some reason he didn't yet fully understand, this idea filled him with a bloodthirsty relish.

"Recce point Babylon," the voice intoned, "on the eve of the Equinox. You can rejoin your existing missions once this is done."

And then again the message became personal, each Clan member receiving their own instructions: "Caracal, you can continue with our efforts to destroy the forests of Madagascar." Caracal started. No one had ever told him that was the mission; he thought he had been providing protection for a businessman!

"Knifefish and Skua, you can continue with our mission to eradicate sharks from the Indo-Pacific." At this, Skua sat up so sharply he bashed his head on the bunk above him. That hadn't been the plan at all! He thought they were here to keep an eye on runaway Captain Panther. All the sharks had been collateral damage. Hadn't they?

One by one, the message addressed the Clan diaspora, spread all over the planet in their destructive cells. The disjointed voice spoke to them, and told them things they didn't want to hear.

In the scrubby vegetation of a huge national park in South Africa, Bear had moved away from the poacher gang he had been living with to watch his message, and his skin prickled with disgust as the Prophet spoke directly to him: "Bear, you are doing exceptional work with the rhino hunt. Every extra rhino you kill makes the species more and more likely to go extinct, and drives up the price of rhino horn still further. Well done, your efforts have made us wealthy beyond all imagining."

Bear had to hold back his vomit. Wealthy? The Clan boys had been brought up from birth to despise money and all it stood for. They lived incredibly simple lives, and had never seen any sign of the Clan making money. Is that what this was really all for? If so, why was he out here in the bush being torn apart by acacia thorns, eaten by mosquitos and shot at by the anti-poaching patrols? Why, when his mission was finished, would he return to a hammock bed in the rain and cold of the ancient forests that were the Clan's traditional home, and not to luxury and comfort? It seemed like he'd been hungry his whole life! Why, if the Clan were secretly loaded? He felt something growing in his belly, that for once wasn't hunger. It was anger.

No, worse than that – it was hatred.

29

From the four corners of the globe they came. They were driven by a mixture of emotions: confusion, bewilderment, outrage, inquisitiveness, savagery, resentment. Their training had taught them how to come and go in silence, blending into any background. Some came across the desert borders, clad in Bedouin robes that obscured their faces.

Sitting at the crossroads of Asia, Europe and Africa, the Arabic kingdom was accustomed to the movement of ancient peoples who know no borders, who see no national boundaries etched in the timeless sands. The nomads of the Bedouin carry no passports, and so as long as Clan boys walked alongside them and their camels, they could be invisible, wandering into the nation by night. Those that arrived by more modern means vanished into the poor quarters of the capital, disappearing among the wanderers and the disinherited. They looked on the ludicrous wealth of the oil sheiks as they thundered past in their limousine cavalcades with fresh eyes, with a discontentment they couldn't yet explain.

When Saker, Sinter and Peregrine had sat hatching their plans, they had found these words in a textbook about dates and the calendar: *The Vernal Equinox is the time of year the sun shines directly on the equator, and the length of day and night are almost equal. In Pagan cultures it marks the beginning of spring, and is a time for change, for regeneration. That's why the symbols of Easter are the egg and the rabbit, for rebirth and fertility. The very word 'Easter' comes from the dawning of the new day in the East, and from the pagan goddess Oestre, the moon goddess of spring. The Vernal Equinox is a time to begin again.* To set right old wrongs. They nodded to each other, it was perfect.

Each Clan boy had the date and time set in their minds, counting down the hours as they begged for pennies on a city street, or plucked edible palm nuts in a far-flung desert oasis. Many had taken to the Palestinian quarter of the city, a jumble of tightly packed crumbling plaster buildings, bleached by desert scorch, with bustling, colourful souks and dark passageways between the buildings. It was the perfect place to be invisible, deliberately dirty heads and faces wrapped in blue or red, or in black and white tassled Bedouin headscarves.

Skua and Fennec passed each other on a bustling market street, but didn't stop, merely making eye contact for a millisecond. An onlooker would have noticed nothing more than two nomads nodding the time of day to each other.

As the day came, Clan boys began boarding buses and sharing taxis out into the desert. Some coaxed a grumbling camel to its feet and began walking, their knowledge of the celestial patterns of sun and stars telling them exactly the direction they'd have to travel in. Bear and Death Adder found themselves on the same bouncing, battered, dilapidated bus, crammed full of chattering villagers, ears assaulted by overloud Arabic music from a crummy cassette tape player. They didn't sit together, or even acknowledge the other's existence. Clan members in the field must be as total strangers, never giving a potential enemy a reason to suspect they were a team.

Their instructions led them to the west, out into the wildest and most arid region of the Jordanian mountains. Here steep-sided canyons cut through pink sandstone rock, the carved rock walls seemingly sliced by the sabre of a jealous god. As the Clan boys crept down the gullies, they saw two-thousand-year-old tombs and temples cut into the rock – the sacred centre of the long forgotten Nabatean civilisation.

As the sunlight faded, the rock turned first orange, then scarlet, then bled blood red before the dusk fell and the stars began to sparkle in a too, too black sky. There is truly nothing like a desert night. So far from light pollution, the sky is blacker than you can believe possible, and the stars shine so extraordinarily brightly it seems you could reach up and pluck them with your fingers. And so quiet! Sometimes the desert is so quiet it unsettles our modern human sense of sound, so quiet it becomes loud, and seems to roar in your ears.

The majesty of the place filled each and every Clan boy with awe as they wandered. Nubian ibex, with their mighty, curved horns, pranced on the rock ridges above them, vultures and kites circled in the last of the sunset light, seeking a place to alight for the night.

As the gully tightened, the Clan boys started to come together, like a crowd filtering into a football match. But this crowd didn't acknowledge each other's presence. Their trained, light footfall meant their passage made no sound. They didn't speak; it was eerily silent. Finally the gorge came to an open chamber. The end wall had been carved into the shape of a temple front, with rounded columns and reliefs of warrior priests, gargoyles and gremlins chipped and moulded over centuries, abandoned for millennia. The twisted faces and snarled teeth of the stone beasts were illuminated by the flickering light of a raging fire in front of the temple.

The boys came one by one, till near a hundred stood shoulder to shoulder before the flames. The walls rose vertically, unscalable on three sides, only the narrow gully behind them as a way in or out. Normally their training would have taught them to avoid a bottleneck like this, an obvious place for an ambush. The entire Clan could have been wiped out with one huge rockfall from above, with one freak flash flood, one single explosive device or strafing machine-gun. But their curiosity overcame their caution.

Something tumultuous was about to happen, and they were drawn towards it, like moths towards the flames.

The crowd stood in expectant silence, staring around them at the walls, at the temple, at the fire. They had never been together in such numbers, never realised how many they numbered. They wore a range of different garbs. Many of them were clad as Bedouin, some were in military uniform, others in simple peasant garb or in the Clan uniform of hoody and combat pants.

Aside from a few more bulky boys, like Bear, or the odd lanky fellow like Serval (named after a long-legged African savannah cat) they all shared the same sleek, sinuous physiques, and had the same explosive, restrained potential about their movements. Fidgety, restless, primed, ready to pounce at the slightest provocation. A few of the boys had grown their hair long to blend in over extended missions, but most shared the same close-cut hair, the same gait, the same dark brows and fierce gaze. They looked like exactly what they were: a band of brothers, made into a lethal and unpredictable fighting force.

In the darkness, Saker gulped down his fear. Sinter took his hand in hers and kneaded his palm, easing away the tension. This was the greatest chance he would ever take in his life. If his plan hadn't worked, he would step out among them and be torn limb from limb. But it was now or never. This was what it had all been working towards. Sinter smiled nervously, and nodded at him. Saker closed his eyes, and breathed in deeply.

"Remember what you always taught me," she said. "The first rule of working with wild animals. Predators can smell fear."

Saker nodded; it was true. Predators target the weak. Old, diseased or baby animals are always the first targeted for food. African game drives will not allow young children or babies on board, because if they start to cry, normally tolerant lions will attack the vehicle. An insensibly drunk man wandering past a wolf pack will be torn to shreds, when they would normally run away. A girl diving with sharks will be ignored, right up until the point she starts thrashing around in frightened panic.

Sinter continued: "To confront a powerful predator, you need to be its equal. You need to show confidence, command, convince them that you are not worth the trouble of attacking, and demand respect. The second your pulse starts to race, and your breathing rate increases, you are doing exactly what prey does. Fear makes you weak. It makes you a target. You will awake their primal instincts. You will become prey yourself."

Saker nodded. The Clan needed to be faced down in exactly the same way as he would stand up to a lion, shark or wolf.

The Clan crowd drew in breath as one as the hooded figure stepped out of the inky hole of the temple door. The dark brown cloak shrouded his shape and concealed his face in blackness. The facets of his hooked nose, brow and chin flickered with the glow from the fire sprites. He stood before them, and raised his hands in the manner of a holy man about to deliver a pagan ritual mass. Every single Clan boy leaned forward, expectant.

Each and every one saw the perfect representation of their initiation ceremonies, when they were first inducted into the Clan as small children. They had all stood around fires just like this, chanting hypnotic rites, shadows casting haunted faces on the walls around them, before being sent baying and panting out into the wilds to show their worth in trials of resilience and hardship. Even now they tasted afresh the hunger of their days running from pursuit, the pain as their pursuers finally caught them and beat them with their fists. The cruelty and brutality of their Rite of Passage would be with them always.

"The masses more easily fall victim to a big lie, than to a small one," the cloaked figure began. He paused, as if reflecting. "Adolf Hitler said that. Who knows why, but it's true. Perhaps because we ourselves tell small lies all the time, but would never think of telling something outrageously, ludicrously untrue because no one would believe us. If *we* wouldn't try and get away with a big lie, then why would anyone else? Why would the people we trust most, who rule our lives, who we look to to show us the way . . . why would they fabricate our world? Even though the facts are there in front of our noses, we will always doubt and waver or think that there must be some other explanation. This fact is known to all expert liars in this world and to all who conspire together in the art of lying."

In the shadows Sinter bit her lip. They'd worked on these words together, never knowing for sure if they would hit their mark. There was a grumble now from the assembled crowd. Who was this hooded man who was lecturing to them? They had expected to be addressed by the Prophet. Where was he? As if to answer their question, a light burst from the ground in front of the fire. Minh had worked long and hard on this projection. It was far more powerful than the one created by the smartphones.

This one was life-size, and was brought into enchanting and ghostly three-dimensional form by the smoke from the fire. It was a real live Pepper's ghost, depicting the Prophet. He stood sternly in front of the crowd, pronouncing voiceless orders, thrashing his arms around with manic, staccato style. The very vision of an insane dictator. The cloaked figure walked up to the projected ghost, and slowly ran his arm through it like a meticulously practised sword stroke. The smoke parted before his hand and the Prophet's dimensions distorted – he became a twisted version of himself, suddenly ephemeral and imaginary.

"It's all an illusion," the hooded man said. "Everything we've ever been told, everything we've ever learned. None of it is real. It is the lie too big for us to ever question."

With that, he reached up for the cowl of his cloak, and dropped the hood down to his shoulders. There was a gasp as one from the Clan crowd. Their enemy, Saker, was suddenly stood there in front of them. An impetuous younger member in the front row snarled and leapt forward to savage his foe, but strong hands reached out to restrain him. A few weeks ago they would already have pounced, but now there was much they wanted to hear.

"We are all brothers by blood," Saker pronounced, "all born of the same father. If you kill me, you kill one of the only family you have ever known. Look at me, look at my face. We are the same! We're not like other people. We follow the same instincts; we're driven by the same impulses. And that's not just our training. It's in our blood."

The Clan remained silent, but he could almost hear their hearts beating. One wrong word now, and they would tear him limb from limb. Overhead, he heard the distant sound of a helicopter, its blades whirring. The timing was perfect, just as he had planned.

"Brothers, we have been taken from our kin at birth. Trained to become killers. We have been told to worship the wild world, then every one of us has been sent on a mission to destroy it. We have never been allowed a normal life, never allowed to know our parents, never known the happiness of a family, or been able to sleep at night without waking in case the assassin's blade is near. We give everything, and then we are no longer viable, and they take us into the woods and slit our throats like spring lambs."

At this there was a gasp. *What?* Clearly none of the boys

assembled had thought at all about what would happen to them once their missions were complete. Another hologram sprang into vision. It was a face that most of them knew well.

"This was Wolf. He was a Clan boy of my age. And this . . ." Now an image of a meadow in the forest filled the space, newly dug soil over his grave. "This is where he is buried. These woodlands that were once our home are littered with the graves of our brothers."

"Prove it!" shouted one boy from the back, and there were general growls of both agreement and dissent.

"I don't need to prove it, work it out for yourselves! Look around you," Saker said. "Do you see anyone here older than me? Have you ever seen a Clan boy in their twenties?"

The grumble intensified. Clearly nobody had.

"Every single one of us here has been trained to love, study and learn from wild animals. And yet every single one of us has in some way been responsible for killing them. We are being manipulated. We have been pawns in a huge game of chess, and the Grand Master is the only one who has benefited."

With that, he swept his hand like a magician, and the Pepper's ghost cleared. In its place came the holograms that Minh had prepared for each individual boy. A vision of environmental destruction from about the planet, designed to shock, to horrify, to awaken. The deep breathing of discontent swelled into a wall of savage fury.

But though the Clan boys were filled with anger for what they saw, there was guilt there too. Every one of them could see their own sins writ large on the canyon walls.

"What does this mean?" one shouted.

"Why are we here?" another cried.

For a second the melee began to build. Saker sensed he had to keep control of the rising anger, or there would be anarchy. He needed to buy some time.

"You're here because I still have faith," he said. "I woke up and saw what was happening to me. So did Wolf. So did Peregrine."

With that, Peregrine stepped from the temple doorway, dressed in the same priestly garb as Saker. "We've decided to set right the wrongs that we created. And if we can, then so can you," Saker proclaimed.

There were new calls now. "As if we're going to trust you!"

"Traitor!"

For a second it seemed the leash was about to be loosed. But then there was a gasp, the crowd parted, and an aisle formed down the centre of it. At the back, behind them all, stood a figure they all recognised instantly.

The Prophet was furious. He had been summoned to the Middle East by one of his most valuable clients. An insanely wealthy sheik, who wanted to hire his boys to ship animals like cheetah and elephant to his sultanate, so he could release them in enclosures, before chasing them down and shooting them in so-called "canned hunts".

The client was lucrative, and the Prophet was not above being summoned. But at the airport he had been met by a helicopter, the pilot knowing nothing of where they were going or what for. And then he had been flown several hours out into the desert, including flying into the night, which most chopper pilots are loathe to do. Upon landing, he had been pointed in the way of the canyon, and then deserted. He had never been treated with such disrespect! And then walking down the dark desert gulch, he had come across this bizarre ceremony, with a pack of howling brigands standing before a fire-lit cult-like druid figure. With that, he realised who the pack was. It was his boys. And the druid . . . was HIM!

With a gasp both astonished and contemptuous, he charged down the gap between the boys to fly at his tormentor. But at the last second he was wrenched back. Many strong hands gripped his arms, preventing his movement. He fought to twist clear, but the more he resisted, the stronger they became.

"You trained them too well," Saker stated.

"I didn't just train them, I MADE them!" the Prophet raged. A vein throbbed at the temple beneath white shaven hair, his ice-blue eyes cold and calculating. "I made you all, and I own you all. You are nothing, you have nothing without the Clan and without me."

"Well, we're doing pretty damn well without you." Peregrine spoke for the first time. The Clan's eyes swung as one towards the new interest. "Since you tried to have my throat slit, I've been happy. Not totally happy, none of us will ever know true, guilt-free happiness, thanks to you. But I am free, and I do what I want, and I don't fear for my life every day. That's as good as any of us can hope for . . . after the things you've made us do."

"And I've been running for years now," said Saker. "I've been afraid every minute. But I've also made friends. I've fallen in love. I've done things I'm proud of."

Sinter's eyes opened wide at this; it was revelation enough that he would feel that way, but she would never in a million years have thought he would voice his feelings like this. Perhaps he really was capable of change after all?

The mood amongst the crowd was as unpredictable as a tempest's winds, swinging backwards and forwards, from hate to horror, from confusion to chaos. Now, Saker believed he could sense longing and a desperate desire for something they knew they could never have: normality.

"The power you are playing with is beyond you, boy," the Prophet hissed. "I have control over my boys. They will eat your flesh, and use your eyeballs for ornaments."

"So . . ." Saker had yet another bombshell up his sleeve. "You would order your children to kill their own brother. You would order them to murder your own son?"

The reaction to this was not what Saker might have expected. Amongst the Clan, it garnered blank, confused looks. But the Prophet looked as if the blood had been drained from his veins.

"Look around you," Saker coaxed the Clan boys. "Look at the brother next to you. We are the same! We look the same, act the same, talk the same. The only difference between us is our connection to our Clan identity. Beyond that, we're nothing but clones. We all came from the same source, made in a test tube, experimented on, our very nature played with, teased and torn apart. We are monsters, made in HIS image."

"You don't know anything!" the Prophet sneered. "The Clan has been here for centuries, and it will be here long after I'm gone."

"Maybe," said Saker, "but without you, it would be something very different indeed."

"So what's your plan, little falcon boy?" the Prophet asked. "There is no prison that can hold me. Do you plan to kill me? You haven't got the stomach for killing, you never did have! You're a coward."

"No," said Saker. "No, I'm not. Cowardice is doing everything you're told, even when you know it's wrong. Cowardice is seeing evil at work, and doing nothing. Cowardice," he was addressing the crowd now, "would be knowing what you know now, and going back to the lives you had before."

The silence was laden with thought, with realisation. It was like the rumbling in the stomach of a dragon who'd been slumbering for an eternity, and was just about to wake.

"You know the story of the Phoenix?" Saker asked. "It refused to eat from the Tree of Knowledge in the Garden of Eden, and was made immortal. But that doesn't mean it gets old and decrepit, then lives for ever, getting more rotten by the day. When the time is right, the bird makes itself a nest, sets fire to it, then throws itself into the flames. In the embers of the fire is found a single egg. That egg hatches, and the Phoenix is resurrected. Before you can be reborn, you have to burn the old order down. Every winter changes to spring. Evolution begins with revolution."

Then, pointing deliberately at his enemy, Saker's voice turned to pure hate. "You have to burn it down. Burn it all down."

With that, the Prophet fought his arms free and leapt for Saker, his fingers like stiletto daggers aimed towards his eyes. Midair, he was ripped backwards and flung to the ground, the air driven from his body. The ice-blue eyes stared skywards in shock for no more than a millisecond, before his prone figure was enveloped in a baying pack of hounds. The Clan boys fell on him like a pack of wild dogs – snarling, yipping, ridden with blood lust, excitement and raw fury.

From the shadows, as the flame-light flickered on the pink sandstone and the gargoyles watched on from above, shrieks and wails echoed around the canyon and off into the infinite darkness of the desert beyond. The impossible brightness of the celestial stars above glittered and gloated.

Peregrine and Saker watched on as their brothers became vicious primal carnivores, and tore their master to shreds.

30

A rusting old converted trawler bobbed like an oversized bath toy on the turquoise waters of a picture-postcard island bay. Snowy white egrets stalked in the shallows, impaling small fish on their rapier bills. Real live dragon lizards as long as a man stalked along the beach, giving the scene a timeless, prehistoric air. Behind the sands, the dry mountains swept up to towering, dusty peaks, their sides rent with rivulets as if some gargantuan monster had scraped its claws down their flanks. Spindly palm trees balanced precariously over the sand, reflected in the gently lapping seas. The name emblazoned down the trawler's side said something of its purpose and mission: *Shark Saviour*.

The injection of funds into their coffers had not made a massive difference to the day to day running of the ship. Granted, the food was a bit better, and they no longer needed to put any time into trying to convince rich benefactors that their cause was worth supporting. Perhaps the biggest change was that they'd had a satellite internet system put on board the boat.

Sinter now sat at the only laptop on board, and looked at the screen. It was an online bank account under her name. Nothing unusual in that. Well, until you scrolled down to the bottom and saw how much money was in there. There were substantially more zeros than one might expect from a teenage Indian girl. Or from anyone other than a dotcom multi-millionaire or a crooked oil magnate. Sinter's fingers hovered over the keyboard.

It was so much money. So much could be achieved with it. But at the same time, it would always haunt her, and create a trail that someone smart would be able to use to follow to her. She didn't want the responsibility any more. Sure, she could still change the world, but she'd do it one person at a time, on her own terms, and without having to spend a life looking over her shoulder and fearing someone was following her.

Amazing that one single keystroke could have such massive import. She pressed the return key, and a status bar came up. *Transferring*, it said, and a small green line started to grow on the screen. The satellite internet was still slow, and it took a few seconds to buffer. But then it clicked in. The status bar disappeared, the transfer completed, the account was empty. She sighed, closed the laptop and walked up on to the top deck.

The ship was pretty much deserted. Most of the crew

were ashore, taking photos of the Komodo dragons, or hiking up to the top of one of the peaks to see the view. Sinter walked to the guardrail, and looked over the side. Despite the boat being moored in quite shallow water, they were on the edge of a submarine trench, hundreds of metres deep. The water below her was a deep, intoxicating blue. An ocean that has no memory, or judgement or concern.

She reached in her pocket, and took out the old phone that Saker had given her. Their parting had been awkward. He had tried to reach for her, but she had resisted. She had been firm. There would always be so much that joined them – outlandish shared experiences she would never go through with anyone else. Life with him had brought thrills and adventure, but also danger and fear. She wanted to go back to her dreams, to training to be a doctor, to care for people; a life of love, wonder and positivity. Mistral had welcomed her back on the boat as if she had been away for years, and as if she never wanted her to leave again. This really was home now. And this old phone was the only link to Saker. The only link to the old life she didn't want to lead any more.

Sinter opened her palm. The phone sat there, seeming to sneer at her. Her mind was made up. Granted, she didn't want to add to the flotsam and jetsam, but just this once, she needed to be sure that there would be no comebacks. Drawing back her arm, she hurled the phone out to sea, and turned before she even heard the splash.

Some hours later, she stood in the same place as the sun began to drop in the sky. The mountains were stained gold with the low light of the sinking sun, the surface of the sea rippled with diamonds and pearls, reflecting the dying of the light. Sinter swung one leg over the guardrail, then the next and, standing three storeys above the Blue, executed a perfect swan dive, arms spread, then coming together over her head to break the surface tension, entering the Blue like a knife, with barely a ripple. She swam down to the drop off, many metres below her.

The Blue invited her, tempting her to explore. As she swam down, her lungs compressed, and suddenly she was no longer buoyant but sinking. Approaching the edge, she found she could stand on the rim, just like being on a cliff top, toes curling over the rock, the void beckoning from beneath. Sinter looked up to the surface above her. The light sparkled, and the silhouette of the ship rolled gently in the swell. Then she looked over the brink, and into the abyss. It was a deep, deep blue, deeper and more intense than she had ever seen before – inky, like velvet, full of stories.

Something down there was tugging on her heart, urging her to swim on further, to explore. Leaning forward, she dived, over the edge, into the depths, and the most intoxicating freedom she had ever known.

EPILOGUE

D awn light cut like scimitars through the canopy of the primeval forests, the morning chorus an echoing, triumphant orchestra. Butterflies began to flutter into life over the pendant yellow merrybells and wood anemones, dog rose and enchanter's nightshade, with its innocent tiny white flowers. Summer was fading, and the sun would soon be a distant memory to these meadows.

A goshawk let loose with an angry kek-kek-kek, its call softened by the mossy trunks and leaf-drenched boughs. Fresh grass shoots sprouted on the dug-over earth. A young man knelt at the side of the disturbed ground, taking care not to crush the new shoots with his feet. To one side, on a crude stick perch, sat a downy bird with a stern look and curved beak. It was a chick, still to grow into the striking plumage that adult saker falcons bear.

The hatchling had been deserted by its parents, but

found in the forest and taken on by a falconer. The chick mewed insistently, trying to tell his surrogate father it was food time. The falconer reached across and handed a chunk of rat to the bird, who devoured it as if it was the last meal it would ever eat.

The falconer held a scalpel-sharp blade with a handle carved from a dropped antler, the brushed metal carved with vines, signs and secret symbols. In the other hand he held between two fingers a thumb-sized chunk of hard wood. Painstakingly he carved the wood, shaping it, caressing the deeply grained material as if it were precious platinum, not a single shaving to be discarded without good cause.

With the basic form carved, he took coarse sandpaper and worked at the surface of the form, smoothing it down. Once that was done, he took a finer sandpaper and then finer still, until finally he buffed the wood to a glossy shine with a finishing cloth. By the time that task was completed, the sun was high overhead, the butterflies were on the wing, and the birdsong had faded to the occasional alarm call from a startled thrush or overenergetic pigeon.

Saker looked at his new fluffy brother, perched on the stick alongside him. He was helpless now, but in just a few months' time the bird would be able to hunt the pigeons, and bring back food for both of them. He reached over to the embers of a fire, and with the cloth wrapped round his hand to avoid burning himself, lifted out a metal rod about the length and thickness of a car aerial. Pressing the red hot tip of it into the base of his wooden carving, he heard a hissing sound as the heated shape was burned into the wood.

Placing the metal branding iron back into the embers, he surveyed his work. The carving was a simple wooden bullet. The symbol had become a warning to enemies of his cause, a warning that they should rethink their actions, or the hounds of hell would descend on their door. Underneath, where the firing cap would be, was the black brand of the head of a falcon. The saker falcon: lone hunter, merciless, ruthless, relentless.

The chick alongside him shuffled and let loose an ugly *caw*, as if approving of his master's work. Nodding his satisfaction, Saker tossed the bullet behind him onto a pile. A pile of identical bullets stacked a metre high, in repeated miniature mountains leading off into the forest gloom.

Behind him in the shadows beneath the trees, the shapes of a dozen former Clan members sat with heads bowed over their work, carving their own wooden bullets, every one of which was both a warning and a statement of intent.

Reaching for his knife and another chunk of wood, Saker began to carve again.